"RICH AND REGAL . . . A VERY GOOD BOOK!"

The New York Times

"The atmosphere, the dreamlike prose, the 'bright animals, ancient names, half-forgotten tales' are what make this book so splendididly worth reading."

The Science Fiction Review

"A book of glowing fantasy . . . the author's imagination is rich, inventive, and far-reaching. The prose style is a sustained shimmering poetry that demands to be read aloud."

The Berkeley Barb

"The best fantasy novel of the year and perhaps of the decade. It's a mythical kingdom fantasy with a marvelous heroine, satisfying strange beasts, and some chilling sorcery scenes."

Locus

The Forgotten Beasts of Eld

Patricia A. McKillip

AVON
PUBLISHERS OF BARD, CAMELOT, DISCUS AND FLARE BOOKS

AVON BOOKS
A division of
The Hearst Corporation
959 Eighth Avenue
New York, New York 10019

Published by arrangement with Atheneum Publishers
Library of Congress Catalog Card Number: 74-75566

ISBN: 0-380-00480-1

First Avon Printing, September, 1975

Printed in the U.S.A.

WFH 10 9 8

For my parents, with thanks

ONE

The wizard Heald coupled with a poor woman once, in the king's city of Mondor, and she bore a son with one green eye and one black eye. Heald, who had two eyes black as the black marshes of Fyrbolg, came and went like a wind out of the woman's life, but the child Myk stayed in Mondor until he was fifteen. Big-shouldered and strong, he was apprenticed to a smith, and men who came to have their carts mended or horses shod were inclined to curse his slowness and his sullenness, until something would stir in him, sluggish as a marsh beast waking beneath murk. Then he would turn his head and look at them out of his black eye, and they would fall silent, shift away from him. There was a streak of wizardry in him, like the streak of fire in damp, smoldering wood. He spoke rarely to men with his brief, rough voice, but when he touched a horse, a hungry dog or a dove in a cage on market days, the fire would surface in his black eye, and his voice would run sweet as a daydreaming voice of the Slinoon River.

One day he left Mondor and went to Eld Mountain. Eld was the highest mountain in Eldwold, rising behind Mondor and casting its black shadow over the city at twilight when the sun slipped, lost, into its mists. From the fringe of the mists, shepherds or young boys hunting could see beyond Mondor, west to the flat Plain of Terbrec, land of the Sirle Lords, north to Fallow Field, where the third King of Eldwold's ghost brooded still on his last battle, and where no living thing grew beneath his restless, silent steps. There, in the rich, dark forests of Eld Mountain, in the white silence, Myk began a collection of wondrous, legendary animals.

From the wild lake country of North Eldwold, he called to him the Black Swan of Tirlith, the great-winged, golden-eyed bird that had carried the third daughter of King Merroc on its back away from the stone tower where she was held captive. He sent the powerful, silent thread of his call into the deep, thick forests on the other side of Eld, where no man had ever gone and returned, and caught like a salmon the red-eyed, white-tusked Boar Cyrin, who could sing ballads like a harpist, and who knew the answers to all riddles save one. From the dark, silent heart of the Mountain itself, Myk brought Gyld, the green-winged dragon, whose mind, dreaming for centuries over the cold fire of gold, woke sleepily, pleasurably, to the sound of its name in the half-forgotten song Myk sent crooning into the darkness. Coaxing a handful of ancient jewels from the dragon, Myk built a house of white, polished stone among the tall pines, and a great garden for the animals enclosed within the ring of stone wall and iron-wrought gates. Into that house he took eventually a fountain girl with few words and no fear either of animals or their keeper. She was of poor family, with tangled hair and muscled arms, and she saw in Myk's household things that others saw perhaps once in their lives in a line of old poetry or in a harpist's tale.

She bore Myk a son with two black eyes who learned to stand silent as a dead tree while Myk called. Myk taught him to read the ancient ballads and legends in the books he collected, taught him to send the call of a half-forgotten name across the whole of Eldwold and the lands beyond, taught him to wait in silence, in patience for weeks, months or years until the moment when the shock of the call would flame in the strange, powerful, startled mind of the animal that owned the name. When Myk went out of himself forever, sitting silent in the moonlight, his son Ogam continued the collection.

Ogam coaxed out of the Southern Deserts behind Eld Mountain the Lyon Gules, who with a pelt the color of a king's treasury had seduced many an imprudent man into unwanted adventure. He stole from the hearth of a witch beyond Eldwold the huge black Cat Moriah, whose knowledge of spells and secret charms had once been legendary in Eldwold. The blue-eyed Falcon Ter, who had torn to pieces the seven murderers of the wizard Aer, shot like a thunderbolt out of the blue sky onto Ogam's shoulder. After a brief, furious struggle, blue eyes staring into black, the hot grip of talons loosened; the Falcon gave his name and yielded to Ogam's great power.

With the crook of an ungentle smile inherited from Myk, Ogam called also to him the oldest daughter of the Lord Horst of Hilt as she rode one day too close to the Mountain. She was a frail, beautiful child-woman, frightened of the silence and the strange, gorgeous animals that reminded her of things on the old tapestry in her father's house. She was afraid also of Ogam, with his sheathed, still power and his inscrutable eyes. She bore him one child, and died. The child, unaccountably, was a girl. Ogam recovered from his surprise eventually and named her Sybel.

She grew tall and strong in the Mountain wildness, with her mother's slender bones and ivory hair and her father's black, fearless eyes. She cared for the animals, tended the garden, and learned early how to hold a restless animal against its will, how to send an ancient name out of the silence of her mind, to probe into hidden, forgotten places. Ogam, proud of her quickness, built a room for her with a great dome of crystal, thin as glass, hard as stone, where she could sit beneath the colors of the night world and call in peace. He died when she was sixteen, leaving her alone with the beautiful white house, a vast library of heavy, iron-bound books, a collection of animals beyond all dreaming, and the power to hold them.

She read one night not long afterward, in one of his oldest books, of a great white bird with wings that glided like snowy pennants unfurled in the wind, a bird that had carried the only Queen of Eldwold on its back in days long before. She spoke its name softly to herself: Liralen; and, seated on the floor beneath the dome, with the book still open in her lap, she sent a first call forth into the vast Eldwold night for the bird whose name no one had spoken for centuries. The call was broken abruptly by someone shouting at her locked gates.

She woke the Lyon, asleep in the garden, with a touch of her mind, and sent it padding to the gates to cast a golden, warning eye at the intruder. But the shouting continued, urgent, incoherent. She sighed, exasperated, and sent the Falcon Ter instructions to lift the intruder and drop him off the top of Eld Mountain. The shouting ceased suddenly, a moment later, but a baby's thin, uncomforted voice wailed into the silence, startling her. She rose finally, walked through the marble hall in her bare feet, out into the garden where the animals stirred restlessly in the darkness about her. She reached the gates, of thin iron bars and gold joints, and looked out.

An armed man stood with a baby in his arms and Ter Falcon on his shoulder. The man was silent, frozen motionless under the play of Ter's grip; the child in his mailed arms cried, oblivious. Sybel's eyes moved from the still, half-shadowed face to the Falcon's eyes.

I told you, she said privately, *to drop him off the top of Eld Mountain.*

The blue, unwavering eyes looked down into hers. *You are young,* Ter said, *but you are without doubt powerful, and I will obey you if you tell me a second time. But I will tell you first, having known men for countless years, that if you begin killing them, one day they will grow frightened, come in great numbers, tear down your house and loose your animals. So the Master Ogam told us many times.*

Sybel's bare foot tapped a moment on the earth. She moved her eyes to the man's face and said,

"Who are you? Why are you shouting at my gates?"

"Lady," the man said carefully, for the ruffled feathers of Ter's wing brushed his face, "are you the daughter of Laran, daughter of Horst, Lord of Hilt?"

"Laran was my mother," Sybel said, shifting from one foot to another impatiently. "Who are you?"

"Coren of Sirle. My brother had a child by your aunt—your mother's youngest sister." He stopped with a sudden click of breath between his teeth, and Sybel waved a hand at the Falcon.

Loose him, or I will be standing here all night. But stay close in case he is mad.

The Falcon rose, glided to a low tree branch above the man's head. The man closed his eyes a moment; tiny beads of blood welled like tears through his shirt of mail. He looked young in the moonlight, and his hair was the color of fire. Sybel looked at him curiously, for he gleamed like water at night with link upon link of metal.

"Why are you dressed like that?" she said, and he opened his eyes.

"I have been at Terbrec." He glanced up at the dark

outline of bird above him. "Where did you get such a falcon? He cut through iron and leather and silk . . ."

"He killed seven men," Sybel said, "who killed the wizard Aer for the jewels on his books of wisdom."

"Ter," the young man breathed, and her brows rose in surprise.

"Who are you?"

"I told you. Coren of Sirle."

"But that means nothing to me. What are you doing at my gates with a baby?"

Coren of Sirle said very slowly and patiently, "Your mother, Laran, had a sister named Rianna—she was your aunt. She married the King of Eldwold three years ago. My—"

"Who is the King these days?" Sybel asked curiously.

The young man caught a startled breath. "Drede. Drede is the King of Eldwold, and he has been King for fifteen years."

"Oh. Go on—Drede married Rianna. That is very interesting, but I have a Liralen to call."

"Please!" He glanced up at the Falcon and lowered his voice. "Please. I have been fighting for three days. Then my uncle tossed a baby into my arms and told me to give it to the wizard woman on Eld Mountain. Suppose, I said, she will not take him? What will she want with a baby? And he looked at me and said, you will not come down from that mountain with the child —do you want your brother's son dead?"

"But why does he want to give it to me?"

"Because it is the child of Rianna and Norrel, and they are both dead."

Sybel blinked. "But you said Rianna was married to Drede."

"She was."

"Then why is the child Norrel's son? I do not understand."

Coren's voice rose perilously. "Because Norrel and

Rianna were lovers. And Drede killed Norrel three days ago on the Plain of Terbrec. Now will you take the baby so I can go back and kill Drede?"

Sybel looked at him out of her black, unwinking eyes. "You will not shout at me," she said very softly. The mailed hands of Coren curled and uncurled in the moonlight. He took a step toward her, and the soft light shaped the long bones of his face, traced lines of exhaustion beneath his eyes.

"I am sorry," he whispered. "Please. Try to understand. I have ridden the late day and half the night. My brother and half my kinsmen are dead. The Lord of Niccon joined forces with Drede, and Sirle cannot stand against them both. Rianna died of the child's birth. If Drede finds the child, he will kill it out of revenge. There is no safe place for it in Sirle. There is no safe place for it anywhere but here, where Drede will not think to come. Drede has killed Norrel, but I swear he will not take this child. Please. Take care of him. His mother was of your family."

Sybel looked down at the child. It had stopped crying; the night was very still about them. It waved tiny fists aimlessly in the air, and pushed at the soft blanket wrapped around it. She touched its pale, plump face, and its eyes turned toward her, winking like stars.

"My mother died of me," she said. "What is its name?"

"Tamlorn."

"Tamlorn. It is very pretty. I wish it had been a girl."

"If it had been, I would not have had to ride all this way to hide it. Drede is afraid the child might declare its legitimacy, when it is older, and fight Drede's own heir. Sirle would back it—my people have been playing for the kingship of Eldwold ever since King Harth died at Fallow Field and Tarn of Sirle held the throne for twelve years, then lost it again."

"But if everyone knows the child is not Drede's—"

"Only Drede, Rianna and Norrel know the truth of the matter, and Rianna and Norrel are dead. Kings' bastards can be very dangerous."

"He does not look dangerous." Her lean, pale fingers whispered over its cheek. A smile strayed absently across her face. "It will go nicely, I think, in the collection."

Coren's arms tightened around the child. "It is Norrel's son—it is not an animal."

Sybel's level eyes raised. "Is it not less? It eats and sleeps and it does not think, and it requires special care. Only . . . I do not know what to do with a baby. It cannot tell me what it needs."

Coren was silent a moment. When he spoke finally, she heard the weariness haunting his voice like an overtone. "You are a girl. You should know such things."

"Why?"

"Because—because you will have children someday and you—will have to know how to care for them."

"I had no woman to care for me," Sybel said. "My father fed me goat's milk and taught me to read his books. I suppose I will have a child that I can train to care for the animals when I am dead."

Coren gazed at her, his lips parted. "If it were not for my uncle," he said softly, "I would take the child back home rather than leave Norrel's son here with you, your ignorance and your heart of ice."

Sybel's face grew as still before him as the still full moon. "It is you who are ignorant," she whispered. "I could have Ter rip you into seven pieces and drop your bloodless head on the Plain of Terbrec, but I am controlling my temper. Look!"

She unlocked the gates, her fingers shaking in an anger that roused through her like a clean mountain wind. She snapped private calls into the dream-drugged minds about her, and, like pieces of dreams themselves, the animals moved toward her. Coren stepped in beside her. He propped the child on one shoulder, his mailed arms protecting its back, one hand cupping its head, while his eyes slid, wide, over the moving, rustling darkness. The great Boar reached them first, fire-white in the darkness, his tusks like white marble that hunters dreamed of, and a sound came, inarticulate, from Coren's throat. Sybel rested one hand above the small red eyes. "Do you think because I care for these animals, I cannot care for a child? They are ancient, powerful as princes, wise and restless and dangerous, and I give them whatever they require. So I will give this child what it requires. And if that is not what you want, then leave. I did not ask you to come with a child; I do not care if you go with it. I may be ignorant in your world, but here you are in my world and you are a fool."

Coren stared down at the Boar, struggling for words. "Cyrin," he whispered. "Cyrin. You have him." He stopped again, his breath jerking through his open mouth. His voice came slow, dredging memory. "Rondar—Lord of Runrir captured—the Boar Cyrin that no man had captured before, the elusive Cyrin, Keeper of Riddles and—demanded either Cyrin's life or all the wisdom of the world. And Cyrin uprooted a stone at Rondar's feet, and Rondar said it was worthless and rode away, still searching . . ."

"How do you know that tale?" Sybel asked, astonished. "It is not one of Eldwold."

"I know it. I know." He lifted his head, his arms tight around the child as a great shape swooped toward them, silent, a shadow upon the night. The Swan folded itself gently before them, its back broad as the Boar's, its eyes black as the night between two stars. "The Swan of Tirlith— Is it the Swan? Sybel, is it?"

"How do you know my name?" she whispered.

"I know." He watched two cats ease through the

night, coming from opposite sides of the house, and she heard him swallow. Tamlorn struggled in his arms, but Coren did not move. The Cat Moriah reached them, nudged its black, flat head under Sybel's hand, then lay down on her feet and yawned at Coren, showing teeth like honed polished stones.

"Moriah . . . Lady of the Night, who gave the wizard Tak the spell that opened the doorless tower where he was captured . . . I do not—I do not know the Lyon—" Gules Lyon, his eyes liquid gold, traced a close circle about Coren's legs, then settled in front of him, muscle sliding leisurely into muscle beneath the glowing pelt. Coren shook his head quickly. "Wait— There was a Lyon of the Southern Deserts who lived in the courts of great lords, dispensing wisdom, fed on rich meats, wearing their collars and chains of iron and gold only so long as he chose . . . Gules."

"How do you know these things?"

The Lyon's great head turned toward Sybel. *Where,* Gules inquired curiously, *did you find this one?*

He brought me a baby, Sybel said distractedly. *He knows my name, and I do not know how.*

"Once he could speak," Coren said.

"Once they all could. They have been wild, away from men so long that they have forgotten how, except for Cyrin, just as men—most men—have forgotten their names. How do you—"

Coren started beside her, and she looked up. The span of unfurled wings blotted the moon, shadowed their faces, then dropped lower, each stroke sucking a heartbeat of wind. Tamlorn kicked restlessly against Coren's hold, wailed a complaint into his ear. The Dragon dropped sluggishly before them, holding Coren in its lucent green gaze. Its shadow welled huge to their feet. Its mind-voice was ancient, dry as parchment in Sybel's mind.

There is a cave in the mountains where his bones will never be found.

No. I called you because I was angry, but I am not angry, now. He is not to be harmed.

He is a man, armed.

No. She turned to Coren, as he stood watching the Dragon with Tamlorn wriggling, whimpering, ignored in his arms, and her eyes curved suddenly in a little smile. "You know that one."

"His name is not so old that men have forgotten it. There was an Eldwold prince taking rich gifts over the Mountain to a southern lord to buy arms and men, whose bones and treasure have never been found . . . There are tales still told of fire blazing out of the summer sky over Mondor, and the crops burning, and the Slinoon River steaming in its bed."

"He is old and tired," Sybel said. "Those days are behind him. I hold his name, and he cannot free himself from me to do such things again."

Coren shifted Tamlorn finally, and the baby quieted. The dark prints of weariness had eased from his face, leaving it young for a moment, wondering. He looked down at her.

"They are beautiful. So beautiful." He looked down at her a moment longer, before he spoke again. "I must go. There will be news of the battle at Mondor. I cannot bear the thought that my brothers may be dead and I do not know. Will you take Tamlorn? He will be safe here, with such a guard. Will you love him? That—that is what he requires most."

Sybel nodded wordlessly. She took the child, holding it awkwardly, and it tugged curiously at her long hair. "But how do you know so many things? How do you know my name?"

"Oh. I asked an old woman living down the road a ways. She gave your name to me."

"I do not know any old women."

He smiled at a memory. "You should know that one. I think—I think if you need help with Tamlorn, she will give it to you." He paused, looking at Tamlorn. He touched the soft, round cheek, and the smile drained from his face, leaving it numb with a bewildered grief. "Good-bye. Thank you," he whispered, and turned. Sybel followed him to the gate.

"Good-bye," she said through the bars as he mounted. "I know nothing of wars, but I know something of sorrow. And that, I think, is what you pass from hand to hand at Terbrec."

He looked down at her, mounted. "It is true," he said. "I know."

She met, as she turned away from the gate, the little round, fiery eyes of the silver Boar in her path. She caught the minds around her, holding them all in their quietness with an effort. *You may go now. I am sorry I woke you, but I lost my temper.*

The Boar did not move. *You cannot give love,* he remarked, *until you have first taken it.*

You are not very helpful, Sybel said irritably, and the great Boar gave a little snort that was his private laughter.

That old woman climbed the wall once, looking for herbs. I snorted at her and she snorted back at me. She could help you. What would you give me for all the wisdom of the world?

Nothing, because I do not want it now. Give it to Coren. He said I had a heart of ice.

Cyrin snorted again, gently. *Indeed, he needs wisdom.*

I told him so, Sybel said.

The next morning, she went out of the house, down the mountain path that led to the city below. The great old pines swayed in the wind, creaking and moaning of the coming of winter. Their needles were soft and cold under her bare feet, stroked here and there with sunlight. She carried Tamlorn, sleeping, in the white wool blanket. He was warm and heavy in her arms, soft and freshly washed. She watched his face, with its long, pale lashes and its heavy cheeks. Once she stopped to nuzzle her face against his soft, pale hair.

"Tamlorn," she whispered. "Tamlorn. My Tam."

She saw a small house within the trees, its chimney smoking. A gray cat curled asleep on the roof, and a black raven perched on a pair of antlers hanging above the door. Doves, pecking in the yard, fluttered around her as she walked to the door. The raven looked down at her sideways out of one eye and gave a cry like a question: *Who?* She ignored it, opened the door. Then she stood motionless in the doorway, for across the threshold there was no floor but mist that moved uneasily, immeasurable at her feet. She looked around, puzzled, and saw the walls of the house looking back at her, with eyes and round dark mouths. The door slipped out of her hand, closed behind her, and the mists moved upward, coiling around the watching eyes, covering them, until it hid even the roof; and the raven flew toward her from somewhere beyond the mists, and gave its question again: *Who?*

Tamlorn wriggled in her arms, wailed a complaint. She kissed him absently. Then she said, standing in the strange, watching house,

"Whose heart am I in?"

The mist vanished and the watching faces hardened into pine knot. A thin old woman in a leaf-colored robe, with white hair in a thousand untidy curls around her face, rose from a rocking chair, her ringed hands clasped.

"A baby!" She took him from Sybel, made noises at it like cooing doves. Tamlorn stared at her and made a sudden catch at her long nose. He smiled toothlessly as she clucked at him. Then she looked at Sybel, her eyes iron-gray, sharper than a king's blade. "You."

"Me," said Sybel. "I need advice, if you would be pleased to give it to me."

"With Cyrin Boar and Gules Lyon to advise you, child, you come to me? Why, what lovely hair you have, so long and fine . . . Has any man told you that?"

"Cyrin Boar and Gules Lyon have never had a baby dumped in their arms. I must give it what it requires, and it cannot tell me. Cyrin said you might help me, since you snorted at him. Cyrin at times makes no sense. But can you help me?"

"Onions," said the old woman. Sybel blinked at her.

"Old woman, I have stood in the eye of your heart while you looked at me, and anyone with such an inner eye is no fool. Will you help me?"

"Of course, child. I let you in. Onions—you grow them in your garden. I was trying to remember. Will you let me have a few, now and then?"

"Of course."

"I love them in a good stew. Sit down—there, on the sheepskin by the hearth. That was given to me by a man from the city who hated his wife and wanted to be rid of her."

"Men are strange in the city. I do not understand loving and hating, only being and knowing. But now I must learn how to love this child." She paused a moment, her ivory brows crooked a little. "I think I do love him. He is soft, and he fits so into my arms, and if Coren of Sirle came for him again, it would be hard to give him up."

"So."

"So, what?"

"So it is Drede's child. I have been hearing about that from my birds."

"Coren said it is Norrel's child."

The thin lips smiled. "I do not think so. I think he is the son of Drede the King. There is a raven at the King's palace whose eyes never close . . ."

Sybel stared at her, lips parted. She drew a slow breath. "I do not understand such things. But he is mine now to love. It is very strange. I have had my animals for sixteen years, and this child for one night; and if I had to choose one thing from all of them, I am not sure that I would not choose this thing, so helpless and stupid as he is. Perhaps because the animals could go and require nothing from anyone, but my Tam requires everything from me."

The woman watched her, rocking back and forth in her chair, rings flashing on her still hands, fire-flecked. "You are a strange child . . . so fearless and so powerful to hold such great, lordly beasts. I wonder you are not lonely sometimes."

"Why should I be? I have many things to talk to. My father never spoke much— I learned silence from him, silence of the mind that is like clear, still water, in which nothing is hidden. That is the first thing he taught me, for if you cannot be so silent, you will not hear the answer when you call. I was trying to call the Liralen, last night when Coren came."

"Liralen . . ." The old woman's face softened until it seemed dreaming and young beneath her curls. "The pennant-winged, moon-colored Liralen . . . Oh, child, when you capture it finally, let me see it."

"I will. But it is very hard to find, especially when people interrupt me with babies. My father fed me goat's milk, but Tam does not seem to like it."

The old woman sighed. "I wish I could feed him, but a cow would be more useful, unless I find some mountain woman to nurse him."

"He is mine," Sybel said. "I do not want some other woman to begin to love him."

"Of course, child, but— Will you let me love him, just a little? It has been so long since I have had children to love. I will steal a cow from someone, leave a jewel in its place."

"I can call a cow."

"No, child, if anyone is a thief it must be me. You must think of yourself, of what would happen if people suspected you of calling away their animals."

"I am not afraid of people. They are fools."

"Oh, child, but they can be so powerful in their loving and hating. Did your father, when he talked to you, give you a name?"

"I am Sybel. But you did not have to ask me that."

The gray eyes curved faintly. "Oh, yes, my birds are everywhere . . . But there is a difference in a name spoken of, and a name given at last by the bearer. You know that. My name is Maelga. And the child's name? Will you give me that as a gift?"

Sybel smiled. "Yes. I would like you to have his name. It is Tamlorn." She looked down at him, her ivory hair tickling the small, plump face. "Tamlorn. My Tam," she whispered, and Tamlorn laughed.

So Maelga stole a cow and left a jeweled ring in its place, and for months afterward people left their barn doors open hopefully. Tam grew strong, pale-haired and gray-eyed, and he laughed and shouted through the still white halls, and teased the patient animals and fed them. Years passed, and he became lean and brown, and explored the Mountain with shepherd boys, climbing through the mists, searching deep caves, bringing home red foxes, birds and strange herbs for Maelga. Sybel continued her long search for the Liralen, calling nights, disappearing for days at a time and returning with old, jeweled books with iron locks that might hold its name. Maelga chided her for stealing, and she would reply absently,

"From little wizardlings, who do not know how to use them. I must have that Liralen. It is my obsession."

"One day," Maelga said, "you will mistake a great wizard for a little wizardling."

"So? I am great, too. And I must have the Liralen."

One evening, twelve years after Coren had brought Tamlorn to her, Sybel went to the cold, deep cave Myk had built for Gyld the Dragon. It lay behind a ribbon of water, and trees about it grew huge and still as pillars vaulting a chamber of silence. She stepped over three rocks to the falls, then slipped behind it, the water running across her face like tears. Within, the cave was dark and wet as the heart of a mountain; Gyld's green eyes glowed in it like jewels. The great, folded bulk of him formed a shadow against the deeper shadow. Sybel stood still before him, like a slender pale flame in the dark. She looked into the unblinking eyes.

Yes?

Thoughts rose slow and formless as a dark bubble in the Dragon's mind, and opened to the dry, parchment rustle of his voice. *It has been a thousand years since I fell asleep over the gold I gathered from Prince Sirkel, and fell asleep watching his open eyes and his blood trickle slowly over coin piece and coin piece and gather in the hollow neck of a cup.* His voice whispered away. There was silence while another bubble formed and broke. *I dream of that gold, and wake to see it, and it is not here . . . I wake to cold stone. Give me leave to gather it once more.*

Sybel was silent as a stone rising from stone. She said, *You will fly, and men will see you and remember your deeds with terror. They will come to destroy my house and they will see gold burning in the sun, and nothing, nothing will turn them back from my house.*

No, said Gyld. *I will go by night and gather it in secret, and if any man watches, I will slay in secret.*

Then, said Sybel, *they would come and kill us both.*

No man can kill me.

What of me? And Tam? No.

The great bulk stirred, amorphous, and she felt the warm sigh of his breath.

I was old and forgotten when the Master woke me

by name in the hollow veins of Eld, and brought me out of my dreaming with his song of my deeds . . . It was pleasant to be sung of once more . . . It is pleasant to be named by you, but I must have my sweet gold . . .

Quick and turning as a snake his thoughts fled away from her, slipping down, down through caverns of his mind to the dark maze of it. Swift as water draining into earth, stealthy as man burying man beneath moonlight, he carried his name down to the forgetting regions where he was nameless even to himself, but she was there before him, waiting behind the last door of his mind. She stood among the half fragments of his memories of slayings, lustings and half-eaten meals and said,

If you want this so badly, I will think of a way. Do nothing, but be patient. I will think.

His breath came once more, and his thoughts welled once more to the dark cave. *Do this one thing for me, and I will be patient.*

She stepped out of the cave, water shining in her hair, and breathed deeply of the cool night air. She thought of the Dragon in flight, smooth flame in motion, and of the deep, peaceful pools of the Black Swan's eyes, and the memory of the Dragon's ground mind with the broken embers of his passions faded deep into her own. Then she heard a rustling behind her in the dark, still earth, sensed a watching.

"Tam? Maelga?"

But no voice, no mind answered. The black trees rose like monoliths, blocking the stars. The rustling faded like the breath of wind into silence. She turned again toward the house, a line between her white brows.

She went to see Maelga a few days later and sat on the skin by the fireplace, her arms around her knees, and Maelga watched her face as she stirred soup.

"There is Something in the forest without a name."

"Are you afraid of it?" Maelga asked. Sybel looked up at her surprisedly.

"Of course not. But how can I call it if it has no name? It is very strange. I cannot remember reading about a nameless thing anywhere. What are you cooking? If I were not already hungry, I would be hungry from the smell of it."

"Mushrooms," said Maelga. "Onions, sage, turnips, cabbage, parsley, beets, and something Tam brought me that has no name."

"Some day," Sybel said, "Tam will poison us all." She leaned her shining head back against the stones and sighed. Maelga's eyes flicked to her.

"What is it? Does it have a name?"

She stirred. "I do not know. I am very restless these days, but I do not know what I want. Sometimes, I fly with Ter in his thoughts as he hunts. He cannot fly as high as I want him to, or so fast, though the earth rushes beneath us and he goes higher than Eld Mountain . . . And I am there, when he kills. That is why I want the Liralen so. I can ride on its back and we can go far, far into the setting sun, the world of the stars. I want . . . I want something more than my father had, or even my grandfather, but I do not know what I want."

Maelga tasted the soup, the jewels on her thin hands winking. "Pepper," she said. "And thyme. Only yesterday a young woman came to me wanting a trap set for a man with a sweet smile and lithe arms. She was a fool, not for wanting him, but for wanting more of him than that."

"Did you help her?"

"She gave me a box of sweet scent. So now she will be miserable and jealous for the rest of her life." She looked at Sybel, sitting still against the stones, her black eyes hidden, and she sighed. "My child, can I do anything for you?"

Sybel's eyes lifted, smiling faintly. "Shall I add a man to my collection? I could. I could call anyone I want. But there is no one I want. Sometimes, the animals grow restless like this, dreaming of days of flights and adventures, of the acquiring of wisdom, of the sound of their names spoken in awe, in fear. The days are over, few remember their names, but they dream, still . . . and I think of the still way I learned, and how only my father, then you, then Tam, ever gave me back my name . . . I think . . . I think I want some days to take that mountain path down into the strange, incomprehensible world."

"Then go, child," said Maelga. "Go."

"Perhaps I will. But who would keep my animals?"

"Hire a wizardling."

"For Ter? No wizardling could hold him. When I was Tam's age, I could hold him. I wish Tam were half wizard. But he is only half king."

"You have never told him that, surely."

"Am I a fool? What good would knowing that do? A dream like that could make him miserable. In the world below, it may even kill him. He is better off playing with shepherd boys and foxes and marrying, when he is old enough, some pretty mountain girl." She sighed again, her white brows creeping into a little frown. Then she straightened, startled, as the door burst open. Tam stared down at her, taut, glistening with sweat, his pale hair sticking in points to his flushed face.

"Sybel— The Dragon—he hurt a man— Come quickly—" He flashed away like a hare. Sybel followed him out. She stood motionless as a tree in front of the house, and caught the current of the Dragon's thoughts with one swift blaze of his name.

Gyld.

She felt him curled in the darkness of his wet cave, thoughts tumbling in his mind of flight, of gold, of a man's pale face staring up at him, open-mouthed, then hidden suddenly behind his upflung arms. She gave a tiny murmur of surprise.

"What is it?" Maelga said, her hands clasped anxiously. Sybel's thoughts came back to her.

"Gyld went to get his gold, and a man saw him flying with it, so Gyld attacked him."

"Oh, no. Oh, dear." Then her gray eyes pinpointed Sybel's face. "You know him."

"I know him," she said slowly, and the frown deepened in her eyes. "Coren of Sirle."

TWO

She and Tam carried Coren into the white stone house, with Maelga following after, long fingers pulling worriedly at her curls. Around them the animals stirred, murmuring, watching. Tam chattered breathlessly, his arms knotted under the weight of Coren's shoulders.

"I was coming down from Nyl's house—we brought the sheep in, and they were crowding together against the fence, and their eyes were rimmed with fear; we did not know why until I looked up and saw Gyld—like a great fiery leaf, a green flame—with gold and jewels in his claws. So I ran home but you were not there, so I was running to Maelga's house when I saw the man watching Gyld—staring at him, and Gyld circled down to him, and the man flung himself down and Gyld's claws scraped across him. I think Nyl saw Gyld— Where shall we put him?"

"I do not know," Sybel said. "I am sorry he is hurt, but he should not have come here; yet it is partly my fault because I should have let Gyld have his gold. Put him there on the table, so Maelga can look at his back. Get a pillow for his head." She brushed a piece of tapestry work off the thick, polished wood and they laid Coren on it. His eyes flickered open as Tam set a pillow under his head. His back, covered with a leather vest, was ripped and scored with claw marks; his bright hair was furrowed with tracks of blood. Tam stared down at him, brows peaked in his brown face.

"Will he die?" he whispered.

"I do not know," Sybel said. Coren's eyes sought her face, and she saw for the first time the light, vivid blue of them, like Ter's eyes. Looking at her, he gave a little smile. He whispered something, and Tam's face flushed.

"What did he say?"

Tam was silent a moment, his mouth tight. "He said it was cruel of you to set the Dragon at him, but he was not surprised. You did not. He had no right to say that."

"Well, perhaps he did," Sybel said judiciously, "considering that I set Ter Falcon at him the first time he came."

"He came before? When?"

Sybel's hands worked gently over Coren's back, loosening torn cloth. "He brought you to me, after your parents died. For that I will always be in his debt. Tam, get some water and that roll of unworked linen. And then stay here to get Maelga whatever she needs." Behind her, Maelga murmured, twisting her rings.

"Elderberry. Fire, water, fat and wine."

"Wine?"

"My nerves are not what they used to be," she said apologetically. Coren, limp under Sybel's careful fingers, whispered painfully.

"Neither are mine."

They finished a flagon of wine among them, as they washed and bandaged Coren, clipped his hair, and laid him to rest on Ogam's long disused bed. Maelga sank into a chair beside the hearth, her hair in wild disarray. Sybel stood staring into the green flames in her hearth, her black eyes narrowed.

"Maelga, why has he come?" she said softly. "It

must be for Tam. But I have reared Tam, and I have loved him, and I will not give him to men to use for their games of hatred. I will not! He is not as wise as I thought if he came here to ask that of me. If he mentions one word of war or kingship to Tam I will— No, I will not feed him to Gyld, but I will do something." She fell silent, the green flames twisting and turning in the depths of her eyes, her long hair falling about her like a silvery, fire-trimmed cloak. Maelga pressed her fingers against her eyes.

"Old and tired," she murmured. "He is finely made, a princeling among men, with the blue eyes and crow-black lashes of the dead Sirle Lord. Those were battle scars on his shoulders."

Sybel shivered. "I will not have my Tam scarred with battle," she whispered. She turned to meet the sudden, piercing lift of Maelga's eyes.

"He could be a very valuable piece in their games. They will not yield easily if they want him badly."

"Then they will have to reckon with me. I will play a game of my own, to my own rules. It may be long years before the Lord of Sirle sees his son again."

"The old lord is dead," Maelga said. "Coren's oldest brother, Rok, is Lord of Sirle, lord of rich lands, walled forts, an army that has threatened the Eldwold Kings for centuries. My child," she said wonderingly. "You have never cried before."

"Oh, I am angry—" She wiped her face with her fingers impatiently. Then she looked down at their glistening. "How strange . . . My father said my mother wept, looking out the windows, before I was born, but I never knew what he meant . . . Why can I not just throw Coren to Gyld and have done with it? But I have his name and the sound of his voice, and the order of his words. He is a fool but he is alive, with eyes to see and weep with, hands to carry a baby and kill a man, a heart to love and hate, and a mind to use, after a fashion. In his own world, he is doubtless valued."

"My child," Maelga whispered. "We are all of one world."

Sybel was silent.

She went to look at Coren before she slept. Tam was sleeping; around her in the dark night she felt the animals' vague night dreaming, colorful and strange as fragments of old, forgotten tales. The white-pillared hall was silent under her soundless steps. The fire slept, curled in charred, pulsing embers. She opened the door softly, and heard the faint, breathless chatter of Coren as he lay burning with fever.

He turned his head to look up at her by the flame of the single, hunched candle by the bed. His eyes glittered like Ter's.

"Ice-white Lady," he whispered. "He was so beautiful, with amethysts and gold in his claws, but they say never, never look upon the face of beauty. And you are beautiful, ivory and diamond-white, fire-white, with eyes as black as Drede's heart . . . blacker . . . black as the black trees in Mirkon Forest where the King's son Arn was lost three days and three nights and came out with pure white hair . . . Black—"

"Arn," Sybel said softly. "How would you know a tale like that? It is written in one place only, and I have the key to that book."

"I know." He blinked, as though she were wavering like a flame. He reached toward her, then dropped his arm with a hiss of pain. "I am hurt," he said wonderingly. Then he shouted, "Rok! Ceneth!"

"Sh—you will wake Tam."

"Rok!" He stirred restlessly, turning his face away from her, and she heard the sudden sob of his breath. Then he was quiet, as she bent over him, touched his hair, smoothed it away from his face. She wet a cloth with wine and wiped his damp forehead again and again until his taut hands loosened and she knew by his breathing that he slept.

She slept late in the morning, then rose, still weary, to check the animals. She walked through the vast sweep of walled grounds to the small lake Myk had built for the Black Swan where it glided proud and silent beneath the blue-gray sky. Wild swan, geese, ducks flying across the mountains from winter had stopped to feed with it. The huge Swan moved toward her as she stood on the edge, its eyes of liquid night. Its thoughts trailed into hers—flute-toned.

Sybel, you are beautiful these days as moonlit ice.

A smile flicked, wry, into her eyes. *Ice. Thank you. Are you well?*

I am. But there are others of us who do not seem so content.

I know. I will see to Gyld.

Who will see to the lordling of Sirle? I have heard he comes to take back what he has given.

He will take nothing from me. Nothing.

So? The great Swan glided a moment in silence. *Once when the child prince of Elon was in danger of his father's enemies, I flew him by night and moonlight where no man could seek him.*

I will remember that. Thank you. She heard a flurry of leaves about her and found Ter Falcon, great talons winking in the pale light.

I smelled a familiar thing, he said, and his clear, ice-blue eyes reminded her again of Coren. *Would you have me drop him off a cliff?*

Oh, no. I think he is damaged enough. I think he has come for— She checked, gazing into the sharp eyes, and her mind emptied swift as water flowing between stones. Ter's feathers ruffled a little in the wind.

I have ridden on the boy's fist and listened to his secret, late night murmurings that he gave to me because I could not answer. I have spent many years in the courts of men and I can guess what the lordling of Sirle has come for.

You will not harm him, Sybel said. *Not unless I ask you. He thinks—he thinks I set Gyld at him.*

What can it matter what such a man thinks or does not think? Ter inquired. She was silent, searching herself.

It matters, she said at last. *But I do not know why.* The Falcon was silent for a long moment. She waited, unstirring, while the winds pulled at the hem of her black dress. Then she felt the wrench at her mind, the sudden, dizzying soar of Ter's thoughts away from her, like the swift Falcon's flight toward a distant sky. But she kept her mind clear, still, her thoughts encompassing his thoughts' flight like a ring that encompassed the earth and the air, growing outward, always just beyond the Falcon's flight; until its flight faltered and broke, and spun downward, downward into a smoldering, fiery inward surge of rage and power that grew in her until her sinews were taut harp strings, and her heart aflame with Ter's hot blood. Yet still, in the center of her mind, there was a cool, endless ring of quiet, holding her own name, that Ter could not reach. He yielded finally, his thoughts retreating like a wave, and she drew a slow breath of the winds. Her mouth crooked in a little, triumphant smile.

Now, why do you even try? she asked.

For the boy's sake. If you had broken I would have killed.

And you are the one that stopped me from throwing him off the mountaintop.

I am sorry, now.

I will not let him leave here with Tam.

Neither, Ter said, *will I.*

The great, black, green-eyed Cat Moriah dropped like a shadow from a tree while she walked back to the house. It padded at her side, and she trailed her fingers through its velvet fur.

There was a spell, the Cat said at last, in its sweet, silken voice, *my former mistress had, that would dissolve a man so completely only the rings on his hands would be left.*

I do not think Maelga would approve of that, Sybel said. *Are you well?*

Maelga has done many things.

She has never dissolved a man. She stopped suddenly, impatiently. *Oh, why even think of it? Neither will I. My father and my grandfather did not like men, but they never killed them. I could not kill a man.*

I can.

Well, he only has to be made afraid.

Cyrin met her at the door, his red eyes guileless under the autumn sun. She stopped and gazed down at him.

What do you think I should do with that man?

The silver-bristled Boar panted gently a moment. *A net of words,* he said at last, *is more powerful than a net of rope.*

So?

So that man is talking to Tam and he has a tongue like a sweet-mouthed harpist.

Sybel's heart fluttered suddenly like one of Maelga's doves. She went into the house and ran to Ogam's room. She opened the door, and Tam's face turned away from Coren, toward her, oddly flushed. His eyes were vague with struggling, incomprehensible things.

"He says—" He stopped, swallowing. "He says I am the son of the King of Eldwold."

Sybel stood still beside the door, while a hot flash of sorrow welled in her and broke and died away. She said softly,

"My Tam, leave him for a while. He must rest."

Tam rose, his eyes clinging to her face. "He says—

is it true? He says— You never told me such a thing."

She reached out to him, touched his brown face. "Tam, I will talk to you in a while. But I cannot now. Please."

He left them closing the door quietly behind him. She sat down on the chair beside the bed and covered her face with her hands. She whispered finally into her palms,

"You told me to love him. So I did, like I have loved nothing else in my world. And now you want to take him from me, to use him in your war games. Tell me now: which of us has the heart of ice?"

Coren was still beside her. Then he gave a little murmur, and his hand pressed, hot, over her hands.

"Please. Try to understand. Are you crying?"

"I am not crying!" His hand fell away, and she looked at him as he lay with his eyes still starred with fever, his back bare to the warm morning light. "And what is it that I should understand? That having given Tam to me to raise and love, now you think you can come as freely and take him back? He does not belong to you—you have no claim to him now, because he was never Norrel's son. He is Drede's son—Maelga told me that twelve years ago. But it is I who have loved him, and I will not give him either to you or to Drede to be used like a piece in a game of power. When you leave here, tell your brother Rok that. And do not let him send you here again. There are those here besides me who have no love for you, and they will not be any less gentle with you next time."

Coren lay lean and loose in Ogam's bed, silent awhile, considering her words. He said at length, "You knew what I came for the moment you saw me. Yet you bandaged my back and cut my hair, so it is too late to try to make me afraid of you. If I leave here without the thing I have come for, Rok will send me back. He has great faith in me." He paused again, then smiled up at her. "It is not only Tam he sent me here to get. I am to bring you also to Sirle, Sybel."

She stared at him. "You are mad."

He shook his head cautiously. "No. I am wisest of all my brothers. There are seven of us—six, now."

"Six of you."

"Yes, and all Drede has is one son he has never seen. Do you wonder he might be frightened of us?"

"No. Six mad men in Sirle and the wisest one you—it frightens even me a little. I thought you were wise that night you brought me Tam; you knew such unexpected things. But in this matter, you are a fool."

"I know." Coren's voice stayed quiet, but something changed in his face, and his eyes slipped away from hers, back into some memory. "You see, I loved Norrel. You know something of love. And Drede killed Norrel. So. In this matter, I am a fool. I know something of hate."

Sybel drew a breath. "I am sorry," she said. "But your hate is not my business, and Tam does not belong to you to take."

"Rok sent me to buy your powers."

"There is no price for them you could pay."

"What do you want, in all the world?"

"Nothing."

"No—" He looked at her. "Tell me. When you look into your heart, privately, what does it require? I have told you what I require."

"Drede's death?"

"More than that—his power, and his hope, then his life. You see how great a fool I am. Now, what do you want?"

She was silent. "Tam's happiness," she said finally. "And the Liralen."

Coren's face startled unexpectedly into a smile. "The Liralen. The beautiful white-winged bird Prince Neth captured just before he died—I have seen it in my dreams, just as I have dreamed at one time or another of all your great animals. But I never dreamed of you. I did not know to. Can you take that bird, Sybel? So few ever have."

"Can you give it to me?"

"No. But I can give you this: a place of power in a land where power has a price without limit and an honor without parallel. Is this all you want? To live here on this mountain, speaking only to animals who live in the dreams of their past, and to Tam, who will have a future that you cannot have? You are bound here by your father's rules, you live his life. You will live, grow old and die here, living for others who do not need you. Tam one day will not need you. What, in years to come, will you have in your life but a silence that is meaningless, ancient names that are never spoken beyond these walls? Who will you laugh with, when Tam is grown? Who will you love? The Liralen? It is a dream. Beyond this mountain, there is a place for you among the living."

She did not speak. When she did not move, he reached out, touched her hair, moved it to see the still, white lines of her lowered face. "Sybel," he whispered, and she rose abruptly, left him without looking back.

She walked in the gardens, blind with thought beneath the red-leafed trees and the dark pines. After a while Tam came to her, quietly as a forest animal and slipped his arm around her waist, and she started.

"Is it true?" he whispered. She nodded.

"Yes."

"I do not want to leave."

"Then you will not." She looked at him, brushed with her hand the pale hair he had gotten from his mother's family. Then she sighed a little. "I do not remember being so hurt before. And I have forgotten to talk to Gyld."

"Sybel."

"What?"

He struggled for words. "He said—he said he would make me King of Eldwold."

"He wants to use you, to gain power for himself and his family."

"He said men would be looking for me to sell—to sell me to my father, and I must be careful. He said Sirle would protect me."

"With what, I wonder. They lost to Drede at Terbrec."

"I think—with you, Sybel, he said there were places for us both, high places in that world below, if we chose to want them. I do not know how to want to be a king. I do not know what a king is, but he said there would be fine horses for me, and white falcons, and—but Sybel, I do not know what to do! I think I will be something different than the one who herds sheep and climbs rocks with Nyl." He looked at her, pleading, his eyes dark in his face. When she did not answer, he held her arms and shook her slightly, desperately. "Sybel—"

She covered her eyes with her hands a moment. "It is like a dream. My Tam, I will send him away soon and we will forget him, and it will only have been a dream."

"Send him away soon."

"I will."

He loosed her, quieting. She dropped her hands and saw him suddenly as for the first time: the tallness of him, the promise of breadth in his shoulders, the play of muscles in his arms hard from climbing as he stood tense before her. She whispered, "Soon."

He gave a little nod. Then he walked beside her again, but apart from her this time, nudging pinecones with his bare feet, stopping to peer after hidden scurryings in the bracken. "What will you do about Gyld's gold?" he said. "Did he get all of it?"

"I doubt it. I shall have to let him fly at night."

"I will bring it—Nyl and I—"

She smiled suddenly. "Oh, my Tam, you are innocent."

"Nyl would not take his gold!"

"No, but he would not forget it, either. Gold is a terrible, powerful thing. It is a kingmaker."

His face turned swiftly. "I do not want to think about that word." Then he stopped to peer into the hollow of a tree. "Last year there was a nest here with blue eggs . . . Sybel, I wish I were your son. Then I could talk to Ter Falcon, Cyrin and Gules and no one —no one could take me away."

"No one will take you. Ter Falcon would not let Coren take you, anyway."

"What would he do? Kill Coren? He killed for Aer. Would you stop him from it?" he asked suddenly, and she did not answer. "Sybel—"

"Yes!"

"Well, I would want you to," he said soothingly. "But I wish he had not come. He is—I wish he had not come!"

He ran from her suddenly, swift and quiet as a cat among the high peaks of Eld Mountain. She watched him disappear among the trees, and the autumn winds roared suddenly at his heels. She sat down on a fallen trunk and dropped her head on her knees. A great, soft warmth shielded her from the wind, and she looked up into Gules Lyon's quiet, golden eyes.

What is it, White One?

She knelt suddenly and flung her arms around his great mane, and buried her face against him. *I wish I had wings to fly and fly and never come back!*

What has troubled you, Ogam's powerful child? What can trouble you? What can such a small one as Coren of Sirle say to touch you?

For a long moment she did not answer. And then

she said, her fingers tight around the gold, tangled fur, *He has taken my heart and offered it back to me. And I thought he was harmless.*

Sybel sat long among the trees after Gules Lyon had gone. The sky darkened; leaves whirled withered in endless circles about her. The wind was cold as the cold metal of locked books. It came across the snow-capped peak of Eld, down through the wet chill mists to moan in the great trees in her garden. She thought of Tam running bare-armed, barefoot through the sweet summer grass and the tiny wild flowers, shouting at great hawks with the voices of rough mountain children echoing his. Then her thoughts slipped away from her to the silent rooms and towers of wizards she had stolen books from. She had listened to them arguing with one another, watched them working, and then she had smiled and gone quietly away, carrying ancient, priceless books before they had even realized anyone had come.

"What is it you want?" she whispered to herself, helplessly, and then as she spoke, she knew that a Thing without a name watched her from the shadowed trees.

She stood slowly. The wind moved swift, empty past her. She waited in silence, her mind like a still pool waiting for the ripple of another mind. And presently, without a whisper of its leaving, the Thing had gone. She turned slowly, went back into the house. She went to Coren's room. He turned his head as she came in, and she saw the dark lines of pain beneath his eyes, and his dry mouth. She sat down beside him and felt his face.

"You must not die in my house," she whispered. "I do not want your voice haunting me in the night."

"Sybel—"

"You have said everything. Now, listen. I may grow old and withered like a moon in this house, but I will not buy my freedom with Tam's happiness. I have seen him run across the high meadows shouting, with Ter Falcon on his fist; I have seen him lie late at night, dreaming of nothing with his arms around Moriah and Gules Lyon. I will not go with you to Sirle to see him bewildered, hurt, used by men, given a promise of power that will be empty, exposed to hatred, lies, wars he does not understand. You would make a king of him, but would you love him? You looked into my heart with your strange, seeing eyes and you found some truths there. I am proud and ambitious to use my power to its limits, but I have another to think of besides myself, and that is your doing. And your undoing. So you will leave here, and you will not return."

She could not read Coren's eyes as he looked at her. "Drede will come for his son. There was an old woman of his court, a highborn lady who swore that Rianna and Norrel never had a moment of privacy—never more than a moment. She tried to help them—they plotted again and again for a single day of privacy—half a night—but always something, someone forestalled them. We took the child at its birth, afraid for its life, and the old woman thought we might kill it if she told the truth, that it was Drede's son. Drede's second wife died childless; he is aging, desperate for an heir, and the woman learned somehow that the child was alive and we did not have it at Sirle. So she told Drede the truth, and now he has a fragile hope. He knows that long ago one of Rianna's family wed a wizard living high in Eld Mountain where few men ever go. What will you do when he comes for his son?"

She shifted uneasily. "That is not your concern."

"Drede is a hard, bitter man. He has long forgotten how to love. There are cold rooms at Mondor he has ready for Tam, a house filled with suspicious, fearful men."

"There are ways to keep Drede out of my house."

"How will you keep the thought of Drede out of Tam's heart? One way or another, Sybel, the world will reach out to that boy."

She drew a breath, let it wither away from her. "Why did you come, bringing me such news? You told me to love Tam. I did. And now you tell me to stop. Well, I will not stop for Rok, or Drede, or for the sake of your hatred. You will have to breed your hate in some other place, not in my house, lying in Ogam's bed."

Coren made a little futile gesture with his hand. "Then guard him carefully, for I am not the only one seeking him. I told Rok you would not come, but he sent me anyway. I did my best." His eyes slid to her face. "I am sorry you will not come."

"No doubt."

"I am sorry, too, that what I said hurt you. Will you forgive me?"

"No."

"Oh." He stirred, his hands moving aimlessly, and she said more gently,

"Try to sleep. I want to send you back to your brothers as soon as possible." She bent over him to check the cloths on his back. He turned, his eyes bright, wavering with pain, and reached up to touch her face, his fingers wandering across it.

"Flame-white . . . Never did one of the seven of Sirle see such as you. Not even Norrel seeing the Queen of Eldwold for the first time as she walked toward him among her blossoming trees . . . White as the blaze of the eyes of the moon-winged Liralen . . ."

Her hands checked. "Coren of Sirle," she said wonderingly, "have you looked into the Liralen's eyes to know their color?"

"I told you: I am wise." And then his smile drained downward, pulling his mouth until she could see the white of his teeth clenched. His hand dropped from her face, clenched. She gave him wine to drink, and wet his face with wine, and changed the cloth on his back, wetting it, and at last he slept, the lines easing on his face.

He left them just as the first snow fell from the white, smooth winter sky. Sybel called his horse, which had been running wild among the rocks, and Maelga gave him a warm cloak of sheepskin. The animals gathered to watch him leave; he bowed to them a little stiffly, mounted.

"Farewell, Ter Falcon, Lord of Air; Moriah, Lady of the Night; Cyrin, Keeper of Wisdom, who confounded the three wisemen of the court of the Lord of Dorn." His eyes moved wistfully across the yard. "Where is Tamlorn? He spoke to me so little, and yet I thought—I thought we were friends."

"You must have been mistaken," Sybel said, and he turned to her swiftly.

"Or is he, like you, afraid of his own wantings?"

"That is something you will never know." She took the hand he offered her as he bent in the saddle. He held it tightly a moment.

"Can you call a man?"

"If I choose to," she said, surprised. "I have never done it."

"Then if you ever have anything to fear from any man who comes here, will you call me? I will come. Whatever I am doing will remain undone, and I will come to you. Will you?"

"But why? You know I will do nothing for you. Why would you ride all the way from Sirle to help me?"

He looked at her silently. Then he shrugged, the snow melting in his fiery hair. "I do not know. Because. Will you?"

"If I need you, I will call."

He loosed her hand, smiling. "And I will come."

"But I probably will not. Anyway, if I want you, I can call you, and you will come without choice."

He sighed. He said patiently, "I choose to come. It makes a difference."

"Does it?" Then her eyes curved slightly in a smile. "Go home to your world of the living, Coren. That is where you belong. I can take care of myself."

"Perhaps." He gathered the reins in his hands, turned his mount toward the road that wound downward to Mondor. Then he looked back at her, his eyes the color of clear mountain water. "But one day you will find out how good it is to have someone who chooses to come when you call."

THREE

The winter closed around them with a cold, strong grip. Great peaks of snow drifted against the house; the swan lake froze until it lay like the crystal face of the moon amid the snow. Ice ran in bars across the windows of the white hall, dropped downward in frozen tears before the door. The animals came and went freely through the warm house, found dark, silent places among the rocks to sleep. Gyld slept curled over his gold; the black Cat Moriah spent long hours drowsing dark and dreaming beside Sybel's fire. Sybel worked in the silent domed room, reading, calling through the black, fiery skies, through moon-colored day skies for the Liralen. She sent her calls, searching and sensitive, across the whole of Eldwold, southward into the deserts, to the Fyrbolg marshes in the east, and the Mirkon Forest in the north, and the silent, unexplored lakelands far beyond the rich lands of the Niccon Lords in North Eldwold. Silence answered her always, and patiently she would call again. Tam moved through the winter oblivious of it, spending days away in the small stone cottages tucked in the curves of the mountain, or lying long and silent with his arm across Gules, staring into the green fire, or hunting with Ter on his arm.

He came one morning in midwinter to the domed room and found Sybel still motionless on its floor, after a long night of calling. He knelt beside her and touched her. She came back to herself with a start.

"My Tam, what is it?"

"Nothing," he said a little wistfully. "Only I have not seen you for days. I thought you might wonder where I was."

She rubbed her eyes with her palms. "Oh. Well. What have you been doing? Have you been with Nyl?"

"Yes. I help him feed the sheep. Yesterday we mended a fence that fell beneath a snowdrift, and then I took Ter into the caves. They seem so warm in winter. And then . . . Sybel . . ." She watched him, waiting, as he frowned at the floor, rubbing his hands up and down his thighs. "I told—I told Nyl about Coren and what he—what he said—and Nyl said—if he were a king's son he would not live up here feeding sheep and running barefoot in the summer. And then—for a while—it was hard for him to talk to me. But tomorrow we are going to the caves again."

Sybel sighed. She rested her head on her bent knees, silent awhile. "Oh, I am tired of all this. Tam, have you told anyone but Nyl?"

"No. Only Ter."

"Then make Nyl promise he will tell no one. Because others might come for you, try to take you away whether you want to go or not. They may try to hurt you, those that do not want to have you king. Tell Nyl that. Tell him to answer no questions of any man he does not know. Will you?"

He nodded. Then he said softly, looking at her, "Sybel, would my father come for me?"

"Perhaps. Do you want him to come?"

"I think—I think I would like to see him. Sybel—"

"What?"

"Is it such a bad thing to be?" he whispered. "Is it?"

She sighed again, her fingers twisting absently through her long hair. "Oh, if you were older. . . . It is not a bad thing, itself, but it is a bad thing to be used by men, to have them choose what you must be, and what you must not be, to have little choice in your life. If you were older, you could choose your own way. But you are so young and you know so little of men—and I know so little more." She drew a breath. "Tam, do you want this thing?"

He shook his head quickly. "I do not want to leave you and the animals." He paused a moment, quiet, his eyes vague as though he looked into himself. "But Nyl—his eyes went so round when I told him, like owl's eyes. And I felt strange to myself. I would like to see my father." His eyes slid to her face. "You could call him for me. He would not have to know me; I could just see him—see what he looks like—"

She touched her eyes lightly with her fingertips, aware of Tam's eyes, intent, hopeful on her face. "If I call him," she said, "it may be that you will have no choice as to whether you stay or go."

"He will not know it is me! I will pretend to be Nyl's brother—Look at me, Sybel! How could he know I am his son?"

"And if he sees your mother in your face? My Tam, he would look once into your bright, hoping eyes and they would tell him more than the color of your hair or the shape of your face." She rose. Tam caught her arm.

"Please, Sybel," he whispered. "Please."

So she called the King of Eldwold that morning in his warm house with its floors covered with rich furs and walls shimmering with ancient, embroidered tales. Three days later he rode with two men through the crusted snow, dark, small figures like brown withered leaves against the white earth. The wind lay frozen in the ice-sheathed branches; their breaths hung in a white mist before their faces. They rode slowly on the winding path upward from the city. Sybel watched them come from her high place as they moved in and out of the trees. She felt the King's mind, powerful and restless, like Ter's mind, filled with the fragment memories of faces, events, with war lust and love, with the cold, black stone of jealousy and the iron core of loneliness and fear like a white, chill, perpetual mist in the corner of his mind. When he neared her, she sent a call to Ter, flying with Tam, to bring him back.

Cyrin brought the message of their coming to her gates. He walked beside her through the snow, his broad back heavily bristled in a silver-white winter cloak.

I saw a man once leap into a pit to see how deep it was, he commented. *But no doubt you are wiser.*

Sybel shook her head. *I am not wise where Tam is concerned.*

It is an easy thing to call a man into your house, but not so easy to have him leave.

I know. Do you think I do not know? But Tam wants to see his father.

She opened the gates of her yard and stepped out to meet the three horsemen.

"Are you the wizard woman, Sybel?" the King of Eldwold said to her. He looked down at her from his black horse, his gloved hands resting on its neck. He was dark-cloaked, simply dressed, as were the two men with him, but she looked into his gray, weary eyes with the web of lines beneath them, and at the relentless stillness of his mouth, and the helm of gray hair on his head, and saw only him.

"I am Sybel."

He was silent a moment, and she could not read the thoughts in his eyes. He dismounted and stood with his reins in his hands, his voice hushed in the great still world.

"Do you know who I am?" he asked curiously. She smiled a little.

"Do you want me to say your name aloud?"

He shook his head quickly. "No." And then he smiled, too, the lines gathering at the corners of his eyes. "You have a little of—of my first wife in your face. You were kin. You know that, of course."

"I know. But I know little else of her family—indeed of anyone living off this mountain. I have nothing to do with men's affairs."

"But that is difficult for me to believe. You would have great power meddling in men's affairs, especially in these troubled days. Has no man ever offered you that power?"

"Are you offering it to me? Is that why you have come up the mountain in midwinter?"

He was silent again, his eyes wandering over her. "Do they not consult you, people from the city—buy little spells, favors from you to heal their children or cows, perhaps? Ease a little life out of a rich kinsman? Seduce a weary husband?"

"There is an old woman, Maelga, down the road who does such things for them. Is it her you seek?"

He shook his head. "No. I came—on impulse. To ask one question of you. Have you heard of a boy livliving on this mountain yet belonging to no one of the mountain? Think carefully. I will pay a great deal for the truth."

"What is his name? His age?"

"He is twelve years old—thirteen, come spring. As for his name—it could be anything." He heard shouting suddenly through the trees and turned. Tam and Nyl ran down the mountainside toward them, laughing, awkward in the deep snow. Tam's light voice came clear across the stillness.

"Nyl! Nyl, wait! I saw riders—"

The King's eyes moved back to Sybel. "Who are they?"

"Mountain children. They have lived here always." She spoke absently, seeing Ter pick up speed, fly ahead of Tam in a swift, dark line toward her. He landed abruptly on the King's shoulder, and she caught his blue eyes and said,

No.

The King stood quietly beneath the heavy talons, his mouth twitching a little. "Is he yours?"

"Yes. He is good protection for a lonely woman." She gave Ter a single word: *Off*, and he moved after a moment to the wall behind her. The King drew a soundless breath.

"I have never seen one of that size. I wonder that you do not fear him."

"Surely you understand power."

"I do. But . . ." His voice softened; a little, frayed smile came into his eyes like moving water behind a film of ice. "I am always a little afraid of those I have even that much power over."

Nyl and Tam, slowed to a silent walk, reached them, their eyes slipping warily over the faces of the King's guards.

"Sybel," Tam said, and Drede turned. "Maelga wants you." He reached out instinctively to soothe the King's horse, a question in his wide eyes, and Sybel said gently,

"This man is from Mondor; he has come in search of someone he lost."

Nyl came to stand beside Tam, his breath pulsing white in and out of the air. The King said to them,

"Do you know of a boy your own age living on the mountain who was not born here?" Nyl shook his head, and the King's eyes flicked to Tam. "Do you? There will be a reward."

Tam swallowed. His hand moved slowly up and down the horse's velvet neck. "No," he said at last. His voice caught, and he said again, "No." The King's iron brows knit a little.

"What are your names?"

"I am Nyl," said Nyl. "This is my brother Tam."

"Your brother? You do not look alike." He touched a strand of Nyl's black hair, fallen across his bony, freckled face, loosed from his cap.

"We never did," said Tam. And then he was still as the King's hand touched his head, pulled back the hood of his cloak to reveal his ivory hair.

Ter Falcon gave a cry behind them. The King lifted Tam's face with one hand and Tam's mouth shook. Then it pulled into a smile that blazed across his eyes. The King closed his eyes. He loosed Tam and turned to Sybel.

"I must speak to their mother. Has she told you anything of her sons? Anything strange?"

"No," Sybel said. "Nothing. They are simple children.

The King's eyes held hers for a long moment. "What do you know of this truly, I wonder, you who know me. I think perhaps I shall come to see you again." He turned, put a hand on Tam's shoulder. "Take my horse. Lead me to your home."

"Our mother is not home," Nyl said suddenly. "She went to help Marte, who is having a baby. Shall I get her?"

"Yes. Go," said Drede, and he ran ahead of them swiftly through the trees. Tam turned the horse, murmuring to it. He gave Sybel one flash of his white face as they left. She turned and went back through the garden into the still house, to the domed room where she sat, her hands quiet in her lap, her eyes unseeing.

Tam came back after a long while. He went to her silently, crept close to her under the fall of her long hair as though he were a small child again. For a long time he was silent. Then he said softly,

"Nyl ran ahead, and told his mother what lie we told the King. So—he left unsure of me. Sybel—"

She felt him trembling. "What, Tam?"

"He—we talked a little. He—" His head dropped suddenly onto her knees. Her hand moved gently over his hair as he cried, his hands crumpling her skirt. He quieted finally, and she lifted his face between her hands.

"My Tam, it is not such a terrible thing for a boy to want his father."

"But I love you, too! I do not want to leave you, but—I wanted—I wanted—to say I was his son and watch his eyes—to see if he was pleased with me. We talked of Ter—he said it was a marvelous thing that I was not afraid to hunt with him." He stared up at her, heavy-eyed, desperate. "I do not know what to do. I want to stay and I want to go. Sybel—If I go—would you come?"

"But Tam, what would I do with the animals?"

"You must come! Bring the animals— Sybel, he would want you to come— Coren wanted you— You could do things for him—"

"Against the Lords of Sirle?" she said a little sharply and he was silent. "That is what he would use me for."

"I do not care what he would use you for," Tam whispered. "I want you to come."

She shook her head, her eyes dark. "No, my Tam. I will do anything for you but that. You have your life to make and I have mine. I am sorry, but you must choose between us. I will always be here in this mountain when you have need of me— No, do not cry, my Tam—" She smiled, her own eyes wet, and wiped the tears from his face with her fingers. "You were so small and soft once," she whispered, "and you fit so surely in my arms . . . I did not know then that you would grow up to hurt me so."

"Sybel, come with me—please come—"

"My Tam—" she said helplessly, and he rose suddenly, ran from her through the house, and out into the yard where she heard his cry to Ter through the softly falling snow.

She rose slowly, went unseeing to the fire and held her hands to it. The Cat Moriah watched her silently, emerald eyes unblinking. Then she put on her cloak and went out, down the path to Maelga's house.

She sat down wordlessly on the sheepskin beside the fire, resting her face against the stones, staring at the flames beneath Maelga's cauldron. Maelga moved softly through her house, doing odd work, while the gray cat wove in and out of her path. After awhile Maelga knelt beside Sybel and put her arms around her, and Sybel's face dropped hidden against her shoulder.

"My child, what is it?" Maelga whispered. "What lies so frozen in your eyes that you cannot even weep?" Her hand stroked the pale, gleaming hair again and again, until Sybel whispered, her voice dry and soft and distant,

"Tam is leaving me. Do you have a spell for that?"

"Oh, White One, in all the world there is no spell for that."

Tam spoke little to her the following days. She saw him rarely as he came to eat and sleep, then left, silent, dark-eyed, with Ter on his fist or Nyl at his side to roam the winter world. She worked little, sitting for long hours with half-finished tapestry on her lap or pacing restlessly before the fire. The animals were silent around her, moving with soft secret steps and still watching through the house and the yard. Finally one gray morning she went to the domed room and stared out at the white, cold world, at the endless, soundless flakes of snow. And there she sent a call down to the city of Mondor to trouble the heart of the Eldwold King.

He came that day alone through the winter. She met him at her gates, with Gules Lyon and the Boar Cyrin watching behind her. The King looked at her, silently, faintly puzzled, and she said,

"I called you."

His face smoothed, incredulous. "You called me?"

"I called you and you came. So my father and my grandfather called the ancient beasts of Eldwold to them."

His head shook once from side to side. "It is not possible," he breathed, and she smiled, her face bloodless in the chill.

"I called you before, so that Tam could see you and choose." His gray eyes narrowed as at a word he had heard but half-forgotten, and she continued slowly, "Twelve years ago—thirteen in spring—Coren of Sirle brought a child to my gates and begged me, for the sake of a kinswoman I had never seen, to care for her child. So I loved that child, and cared for him, and watched him grow, and now . . . at his wish, I have called you to return him to the world of men."

The King's eyes closed. He sat still, the snow catching on his face, on his shoulders, and she saw the breath move out of him in a long, slow, white mist. He dismounted.

"Where is he?" he whispered.

"Out, with Ter Falcon. I will call him back soon, after we have talked a little." She opened the gates. "Come to my hearth. You are cold. And I am cold, too, a little."

He followed her in. She put another chair beside the fire for him. He untied his cloak and dropped it wet on the stones and held his hands to the blaze. They trembled, and he dropped them and sat.

"Tam," he said softly.

"Tamlorn. Are you pleased with him? He wanted you to be."

He smiled wonderingly, the worn mask of his face loosening. "How can he doubt that? He is so tall, so strong and free-voiced, with his mother's hair and her eyes . . ."

"No, I think they are your eyes," she said judiciously and his smile deepened, caught in his eyes like sunlight in a pool. He reached across the distance between them and took her hand between his own long, scarred hands.

"How can you give him to me?"

She drew a breath. "How can I not, when he wants you?" she whispered. "I do not want to give him to anyone—anyone, because I think he will be troubled by powerful men, by things he does not understand. You will make a king of him, and he will learn much of hatred, lies and things that lie nameless in the deep pools of men's hearts. But he looked at you, and I saw his smile. He is your son. He is nothing to me. I have loved him for twelve years, and you for—twelve minutes, but I cannot hold him here. I can hold a great Falcon and an ancient powerful Lyon, but I cannot hold one sweet-eyed boy against his own wantings."

His gray brows knit a little as he listened. "You are so strange, Sybel. You ask nothing from me and yet you surely must know how desperate I was for him."

"There is nothing you have that could have bought Tam from me," she said swiftly.

"Perhaps. Powerful men have been looking for him to sell him to me. They are not so kind to an old, scarred lion. Ask me—anything. Anything."

"Only love him," she whispered. His fingers tightened.

"I am sorry," he said, and she shook her head.

"No. Be happy. It is a good thing to have a child to love. He is a very loving boy and he likes powerful things, which is why, I think, he was drawn to you. You are a little like Ter."

"Ter?"

"The Falcon."

"Oh." He smiled, the hardness melting from his eyes, his mouth. He lifted one hand toward her, then dropped it, and memories filmed his eyes. "Rianna had such white skin . . . Rianna. I have not spoken her name for twelve years. Silent out of anger . . . then silent out of grief. She was a sweet, warm wind in my heart, a resting place, a place of peace where I could forget so many things . . . And then I saw her give a look to Norrel one day, a look like the touch of a mouth. And so, I lost my still moment of peace. Here, sitting in your quiet house, I have found a little of it again."

"I am glad," she said gently. "And I am so glad that—" She checked, a little color in her face.

"Glad of what?"

"That—Coren Sirle was wrong. He said you were a bitter man with no love left in you. But I think you will love Tam."

The smile went from his eyes. "Coren," he said tonelessly. "He came here. For Tam?"

"Yes."

"You did not give Tam back to him. Yet I have heard of his clever tongue and his sweet smile."

The flush deepened around her eyes. She said tartly, "Do you think I have so little love for Tam that I would give him to the first sweet-voiced man who came wanting him? I would not have given him to you if I thought he could not love you."

"You would have let me die heirless?"

"What concern of mine are your affairs? Or Coren's? What kind of peace would there be in me or in my house if I took interest in the wars and feuds that you weave in the courts below? I do not understand such things. I understand only what lies within my walls."

His eyes were still, a little hard on her face, as though he were seeing her for the first time. "And yet you are so powerful . . . You drew me without my will out of my house—you could do anything you chose with me and I could not fight you. Did Coren of Sirle seek you as well as Tamlorn?"

"Of course," she said steadily. "He asked me the price of my powers."

"And."

"And I told him. I want Tam's happiness. I want a white bird with soft, trailing wings. He could not give me either. So he left me."

Drede eased back in his chair. Sybel watched him silently awhile. The melted snow streaked the gray mane of his hair to the sides of his dark, lined face; fire coiled in a blue stone on one strong, taut hand. He sensed her watching finally, turned suddenly to meet her eyes.

"What are you thinking?"

"Of Gules Lyon. And the Falcon. And a little of the Dragon . . ."

He smiled. "So you also are drawn to powerful things."

She looked away from him, startled, and felt her face slowly warm with blood. He leaned forward, and she felt in his nearness a disturbing, unfamiliar power. His fingers touched her face lightly, turned it back to him.

"Come with us. Come back to Mondor with Tamlorn and me."

"To work for you against Sirle?"

"To work with me, for Tamlorn. Bring your animals, so there will be whatever you love at Mondor. We will make a king of Tamlorn. Come. And, if you like, I will make of you a queen."

The blood beat, hot in her face. "It is more than Coren offered me," she murmured, and suddenly she rose, turned away from him and felt around her the cool, white walls. "No."

"Why?"

"I do not know. But, no. I could not—I could not work against Sirle."

"So."

She looked down at him quickly. "It has nothing to do with Coren. I do not want to choose which one of you I must love or hate. Here, I am free to do neither. I want no part of your bitterness. You do not have to be afraid of me. I would never work with the enemies of Tam's father. You are safe from me. And so is Sirle, because I will not take your hatred as my own."

He was silent, his brows drawn, and she could not see his eyes. "You are too powerful," he murmured, "and too beautiful . . . You are an uncomfortable thought. But I believe you. You would not work against Tam." He rose, too, restlessly, then turned at the sound of the door opening. Tam stood shaking the snow off his cloak. He closed the door and came toward the fire and saw them.

He stopped. The blood flared into his face. Drede held out his hand.

"Come."

He was still a moment, his eyes flicking back and forth uncertainly between their faces. Then Drede smiled and Tam smiled back slowly, swallowing. He came to them, stood between them, holding his hands to the blaze. Drede said softly, "Look at me," and he turned to meet the King's eyes.

"Give me your name."

"Tamlorn."

"And your mother's name."

"Rianna."

"And your father's."

His mouth twitched, steadied. "Drede."

He rode back that afternoon with the King. Sybel

watched them leave from her gates. The snow had stopped falling; the world was soundless but for their quiet voices. Tam stood before her wordlessly a long moment, while the King waited, mounted behind him, and she looked smiling, her eyes wet, into his eyes. She touched his face, smoothed a lock of hair away from his eyes. Then she said,

"Tam, I have a gift for you."

She spoke Ter's name and the great Falcon came to settle on Tam's shoulder. He started.

"No—Sybel, he will miss you."

"No. He is a king's bird. And if you ever are in danger he will protect you, and when I call his name, he will tell me from far away that you are well and happy." She lifted her eyes to Ter's blue eyes, and for a moment he said nothing to her. Then words came.

I did not think there would be a place for me again in the world of men.

There is one place, she said. *Guard him well and wisely.*

I will, greatest of Heald's children. And if ever you need me, call, and I will come freely.

She smiled. *Farewell, my great Lord of Air.*

Tam hugged her so tightly that the mist of their breaths in the chill air stilled. Then he mounted behind Drede, the Falcon on his arm. Drede bent low, took Sybel's hand.

"There will always be a place for you with us if you choose it. And if you do not, there is one place in my heart where your name will be, in silence." He held her hand a moment against his mouth. Then he turned the dark horse onto the mountain path, and Sybel watched until Tam's face, turned always toward her, was lost among the trees.

She turned, shivering a little, and went back into the garden. The snow began to fall, light, silent, endless. Gules Lyon appeared silently beside her; she trailed her hand absently through his mane. She went into the quiet, darkening house and sat down before the fire. Moriah came to rest at her feet. She sat there while the fire crept into embers and pulsed within them secretly, and while they burned themselves to blackness, and the night fell, cold, around her, and the snow fell across her threshold, blotted the last footprints of Tam, and the crescents of the prints of the King's horse. That night, the next day, and the next night she sat there, hands motionless on the arms of her chair, her eyes unwavering, as if she could still see the dancing green flame, and the white hall was cold and silent about her.

She stirred finally, blinking. She saw her animals about her, even the fiery mass of Gyld, curled silent on the stones, and the beautiful, secret-eyed Swan watching her from the doorway of the domed room. She turned and found Cyrin's red eyes behind her. She smiled a little, her mouth stiff in the cold.

"I am here. Are you hungry?"

Her voice faded, unanswered, among the stones. Then Gules Lyon pushed beneath her hand.

Get up, he said. *Tend the fire. Eat.*

She rose, sighing, and knelt before the hearth. Then her hands checked, wood-filled, over the grate. She turned, feeling the nameless Thing with her among the animals. She searched for it, her eyes narrowed, in the shadowed corners, behind the folds of tapestry. It stood just beyond her eyesight, just beyond the circle of her mind, formless, nameless. A thought, the sudden pulse of a memory, flicked through her head. She put the wood down and went into the domed room. She unlocked a huge, gold-leafed book, one of Ogam's, with parchment pages of ancient writings, the collections of forgotten tales as old as the reign of the third King of Eldwold. She leafed through the pages, searching for a few brief lines, and found them finally. She sat down on the floor, the heavy book on her lap, and read silently:

> And there is that fearsome monster, which awaits men around dark corners, through dark doorways, in the blackest hours of the night. Only the fearless survive looking upon it. It is called Rommalb, when spoken of, for to speak its name truly is to summon it.

She smiled slowly. "Rommalb," she said aloud, and turned the name around on her tongue. "Blammor." And looking up, she saw it finally.

FOUR

It was a shadow in the shadows, a black mist taller than she, with eyes like circles of sightless, gleaming ice. She closed the book and slowly rose to face it. She touched its mind and found it as still, as dark.

Give me your name.

Its mind-voice was a rustle of dried leaf. *Blammor.*

Why have you come to me so freely? Most struggle to hide their names. But you came uncalled.

I was not uncalled. And you have a strange power, that draws me and that is to see me as I am truly. Therefore I came to you, and I will serve you, as one day you will serve that one who sees you truly.

Do I see you truly now? A black mist with fire-white eyes, sightless yet seeing?

That is part of me.

You fascinate me, she said. *Do all men see you this way? There are tales of your terribleness.*

Men see what they are most afraid of.

What do you require of me?

Nothing, it said, *but your fearlessness. I will go now. I have night work.*

It faded into the shadows. They trembled a moment at its passing.

She turned, rubbing her chilled arms, a little smile crooking her mouth. She went to the hearth again and lit a taper from the green flame burning steadily on the mantel. The fire danced in a few moments from the hearth, and she lit candles from it, and torches, moving softly to place them in the chilled room, while the half-lit forms of Swan, Boar and Lyon watched her silently. Then, faint through the singing winter winds, she heard a shouting at her gates.

Her white brows knit a little, puzzled. She called Ter, then remembered he had gone, so she took Cyrin out with her, and a fiery torch that set the deep snow ablaze about her. The flakes fell in huge, great wheels of intricate crystal that vanished in the torch flame. A man stood cloaked, hooded at the gates, his horse behind him. She moved the torch to light his face behind the bars and beneath the hood his hair flamed.

She sighed. "Oh." She unlocked the gates, and he stepped into the yard. "Take your horse to the shed on the side of the house; I will keep the others out."

"Thank you," he said, the words blowing white in the wind. His shoulders were cloaked with snow that melted in dark trails down his back as he took the torch from her.

He joined her a few moments later in the house. He nodded courteously to Gules as he passed, and to Moriah, curled like a shadow. Sybel took his sodden cloak, hung it to dry beside the fire, and he stood at the hearth, drinking the flame, shuddering.

"That was a long, cold ride from Sirle. Sybel, your house is chilled. Have you been away?"

"No. I have been . . . I do not know where I have been, but I do not think I have come back yet." She sat down again, spread her hands to the fire. "Why have you come? You must know by now that Tam is with Drede."

"I know," he said. "I came because you called."

She stared up at him in amazement. He smiled, his chilled face taking color from the warmth, his lean hands cupping the blaze.

"I did not."

"I heard you. Sometimes, in silence, at night, I hear the voices of things beyond eyesight, like echoes of ancient songs. I heard your voice, lonely in my dreams—it woke me, so I came. You see, I know how it is when you speak a name into an empty room with no one on earth to answer to it."

She was silent, her mouth open, wordless. He sat down beside her. Moriah rose leisurely, came to lie at their feet and stare at him out of green, inscrutable eyes. Sybel drew a breath and closed her mouth.

"I have never heard of such a thing. What are you? You are a fool in some ways, and yet you know other things that amaze me."

He nodded, the smile tugging deeper at his mouth. "The seventh son of Lord Steth of Sirle, my grandfather, had seven sons, and I am his youngest. Perhaps that is why I hear things the trees tell as their leaves whisper at moonrise, or the growing corn tells, or the birds at twilight. I have good ears. I heard the silence of your white walls even in the noisy halls at Sirle."

She looked away from him to the fire. "I see," she said softly. "I did need someone, but I did not know it until now. Are you hungry?"

"Yes. But sit still a while, and when I get warm, I will cook something."

"Can you cook?"

"Of course. I have been alone many times in lonely places with only the cry of a marsh bird or a hawk to answer me when I talked."

"You have five brothers. Why would you need to go alone?"

"Oh, they hunt with me. But when I need to travel to some forest or lake spoken of in an old tale, to listen to that secret place—they cannot get excited about such things. Once I went to Mirkon Forest, the great black forest north of Sirle, with trees like black stone, and roots dark and swollen above the earth, and I listened to one single falling leaf and I heard the whisper of Prince Arn's name as it fell."

A corner of her mouth went upward in her tired face. "So Maelga used to tell Tam such tales at night, when he was little and troubled."

"Sybel, Rok mocks me when I tell him such things. And Eorth, who is a great, witless dragon, grins at me and hugs me until my bones crack. But I did not think you would laugh at me."

Her dark eyes slid, hesitant, curious, to his face. "I am not laughing at you. But it crossed my mind that you might have come, that your brother might have sent you, to see if I were pledged to help Drede, since I gave Tam to him. Drede—Drede was a little afraid of me, because I called him here—"

"You called him?"

"Yes, but only to give Tam to him, nothing more. I did an unwise thing: I told him you had come here, too. So he is unsure of me, as now I think your brother Rok must be, too."

"Oh, yes." He smiled wryly, but his red brows were knit. "Where was Cyrin or Gules to give you advice? You are wise in things beyond men's knowledge, but it was not wise to call a king insecure in his power, and draw him to you without his knowledge."

"I told him he had nothing to fear from me."

"And that reassured him, I suppose."

"I doubt it." Then she shook her head. "Oh, but why should it matter to me what he thinks of me, or what the Lord of Sirle thinks. Did Rok have anything to do with your coming?"

"I told you why I came." His smile had gone, but his

light eyes were steady on her face. She made a little, restless gesture.

"Yes. But how you would hear my lonely voice above all the voices in Eldwold, I do not know."

"I know," he said. "I love you."

She opened her mouth to reply, but found suddenly she was wordless. Coren watched, a touch of color on the high bones of his face; when she laughed finally, his face flamed.

"Well. Drede offered to make me Queen of Eldwold —what have you to offer me?" She folded her hands on her lap and looked up at him, and found his eyes shocked, ice-blue.

"Drede," he whispered. "Drede." His clenched hands opened, closed on his knees. He drew a deep, soundless breath.

"Did you laugh like that at him?"

"No," she said, surprised, and he rose abruptly. She heard the circle of his restless steps on the stones behind her. Then they came back to her.

"I thought of you with your hair silver as snow all through that cold, slow journey from Sirle," he whispered. "I felt you troubled, deep within me, and there was no other place in the world where I would rather have been than in the cold night, riding to you. When you opened your gates to me, I was home. I did not know you would hurt me so."

Her lips parted as she heard the echo of her own words. Then she looked down at her taut, folded hands.

"I am sorry. But, Coren, I cannot—I cannot trust you."

"I see."

"I— When I look at you, I see the shadow of your hatred, the shadows of your brothers behind you, wanting me, wanting to use me. You must—surely you must understand that."

"Yes."

Her eyes flickered up to him. He stood motionless beside her chair, his face still, colorless. She shifted a little, uncertainly. Then she touched his arm.

"Sit down. We are both tired and hungry. I have not slept since Tam left, and I am tired of arguing."

"Sybel—" He stopped. He sat, not looking at her. He said after a moment, "If I swore—if I swore by my love for Norrel that I would never try to use you, or let anyone else use you against your will—if I swore that, would you begin to trust me a little?"

"Could you swear that?"

He met her eyes and nodded. "Yes. I will think of a way to kill Drede without involving anyone."

"You will not!"

"But, Sybel, what am I to do?"

"You have five other brothers—be content with them."

"I will not! I cannot—Sybel, Norrel—when I was younger, and so unsure of myself, of my strange knowledge—Norrel of all of them never laughed at me. I could tell him that in the Fyrbolg marshes I had seen the ghosts of men who died chasing the White Stag that the wizard Tarn had shaped out of smoke, and he would believe me. He would not understand, but he would believe me. He taught me how to ride, how to fight, how to hunt with a hawk. When he fell in love with Rianna, I fell in love with her, too, wanting her for him. When Drede killed him at Terbrec, I saw him fall. I could not—I could not reach him in time, so he died with no one beside him at a battle that was fought for him. That is what I cannot forgive Drede: that Norrel died alone, without help, without comfort."

His voice faded. A branch snapped in the fire; the wind murmured restlessly beyond the walls, moving in the darkness around her house like a beast seeking entrance. She said finally, haltingly,

"I am sorry. But Tam loves Drede. So—I do not want Drede killed."

She heard his slow, indrawn breath. "So. Ice-white Lady, what shall I do? I cannot stop either my loving or my hating."

"I do not know what you should do. I know nothing of hating, and only a little of loving. I wish—I wish I could ease your sorrow, but I cannot."

"You could. I think you could."

"No."

He sighed. Then his fingers dropped, curled gently over her folded hands, and she raised her head.

"It took a great love to give Tam to Drede. I hope he is happy with Drede, for his sake, and yours, though I cannot understand how Tam would prefer Drede to you."

She smiled, the green light gleaming in her hair, on her weary face. "Tam is drawn to people who need him." She paused. "Surely—surely there is some woman of your own world who has such a need of you. You are gifted, and kind, and—very—and pleasant to look at."

"Thank you," he said gravely. "Why is that so hard for you to say? It is so easy for me to say that you are wise, magical, honest, very beautiful to look at, and I love you." He touched a strand of her ivory hair. Then he shook his head quickly at her restless movement. "I will not—I will not trouble you with things you do not want to hear from me now. But if—if you could give me something of friendship, it would ease me."

She looked at him, her face opening a little to him. "You came tonight, when I needed some kindness. For that, I am in your debt."

"Good." He rose, put more wood on the fire, the flame dancing pale over his face. "Sybel, your fire is the color of young trees . . . I will cook some supper now— No, stay here. Trust me in your kitchen. Sleep a little, if you can."

He left her quietly, and as quietly, Cyrin Boar rose from the shadows and followed him into the kitchen. Investigating, Coren discovered her knives, and pots, the loops of sausages on her rafters, new-made bread, and chilled vegetables from her garden. He stripped a carrot at the cutting board, and began slicing it. The great Boar remarked behind him in its golden voice,

"The trained falcon returns to its master's hand eventually."

Coren's knife slipped, struck hard at the cutting board. He turned. "I had forgotten that the Lord of Wisdom had a voice to speak with."

The small red eyes regarded him, unblinking. "What would you give me for all the wisdom of the world?"

"Nothing." He turned back to his work. "I have heard you know the answers to every riddle save one. That will be the one I need answering."

Cyrin snorted gently. "The wise man knows the riddle to ask it."

"And that the asking and answering are one." He swept the chopped carrot into a pot, and began peeling a potato. "You mistrust me. I am no trained falcon bound by the leash of Rok's politics. He had nothing to do with my coming."

"When the Lord of Dorn received in secret from the witch Glower the death spell she made for his enemies, a shadow darker than night stood beside him, bound to him."

Coren was silent, slicing the hard potato into rings. He said finally, "It is not to you I must prove I can love freely, but to Sybel."

"Her eyes see clearly through darkness."

"I know. I have hidden nothing from her."

"Roots are grown in darkness."

"So they are." He inspected another, and peeled it.

"But I do not think, like a root grows, in secret."

"The giant Grof was hit in one eye by a stone, and that eye turned inward so that it looked into his mind, and he died of what he saw there."

Coren's head turned sharply. The silver-gray Boar stood panting mildly in the doorway.

"If that is a riddle, I do not know the answer."

The sweet-mouthed Boar considered. "Then I will tell you. Ask Sybel what name she spoke today before she spoke yours."

Coren's red, straight brows flicked into a frown. "I will," he promised, and reached for a pale length of parsnip.

He brought a rich soup and hot spiced sausage, thick-crusted bread and cups of heated wine to her, and found her sleeping, her hands limp in her lap. She half woke as he pulled a small table between their chairs, and he spoke her name gently.

"Oh." She straightened, rubbing her eyes with her fingers.

He gave her wine. "I am glad you slept a little."

"It was good. I did not dream." She sipped wine, color returning to her face. "Your soup smells like Maelga's."

He served her, then sat down beside her with a bowl on his knees. "You should not go so long without eating."

"I forget to. Coren, this is good. I do not know which is warmer in me, your kindness or your soup."

He smiled. "It does not matter. Cyrin came to talk to me while I cooked."

Her brows rose. "He did? He speaks so rarely. What did he say?"

"He gave me a riddle. When I could not answer it, he told me to ask you what name you spoke today just before mine."

"Why? Is that the answer?"

"I think so. Whose name was it?"

She thought, frowning. "Oh. It was the Blammor's name, but I do not see—" She stopped abruptly, her eyes widening. Her voice flashed sharp with anger. "Cyrin!" Coren's plate crashed full at her feet as he rose.

The Blammor appeared before them, the green flame dancing dimly through it. Its crystal eyes stared into Coren's, and he stood motionless, voiceless, his face the color of ice. Imperceptibly as a mist, the Blammor moved, lengthening, widening, until it hovered like a shadow over Coren, so close his bloodless face seemed smudged and limned with darkness. A sound broke from him, sharp, incoherent, and he swayed gently, as though he were held upright by a wind. Then Sybel, her hands clenched cold against her mouth, heard his whisper.

"Blammor . . ."

The Blammor turned its eyes to Sybel.

Is there anything more? it asked indifferently, and she shook her head.

"No," she whispered. It melted away; the fire sprang, warm into her face.

Coren's head dropped into his hands. He covered his hands with the heels of his palms, ground them against his eyes as though to rub away a vision. He fell, so suddenly she could not catch him; she knelt beside him, helped him sit.

"Coren—" He did not answer. She reached desperately for wine, and saw, watching beyond the circle of light, the red, imperturbed eyes of Cyrin. She sent the blaze of a furious cry into his mind.

I would have sent him on his way—there was no need—

"Sybel—" Coren's voice came to her as from a deep place within him. She turned to him, her hands closing on his cold, taut fingers.

"I am here."

"Hold me. Hold me tightly."

She put her arms around him, held him so close she could feel the leap of his heart and the long shudderings of his breath.

"I am sorry. I am sorry," she whispered, and kissed him as though he were Tam come to her for comfort. Then a thought stirred in her mind, and she drew away from him. He murmured a protest, his hands dropping from his eyes to pull her back. She said sharply,

"Coren."

He opened his eyes, dazed, as though he were coming out of a dream. "What?"

"Coren, how did you know Rommalb's name?"

He gazed at her, his hands limp on her shoulders, his face drawn, white. She moved his hands, held them tightly as she sat with him on the floor. He said finally,

"I know it."

"But, Coren, how?"

"How do I know anything?" He leaned back against the stones, closing his eyes.

"But how?"

"I had to know." His words lay strengthless a moment between them. "I would have died on your hearth," he whispered. "I have been in one great battle, I have fought unexpectedly at night, alone, but I have never—I have never before seen death come at me so certainly as at your hearth. It was the color of night, and I could not breathe because it was airless, and I knew—I knew if I could find a name, put a name to it, it could not harm me. All my thoughts shouted of death—flew in circles like frightened birds—but I knew it could not be death, in your house, at your hearth. So a part of me searched for a name among all the ancient names I have known. Then I knew what it was. It was not death but fear. Rommalb. The fear men die of." He opened his eyes, looked at her from some nameless place. "Sybel, I could not let myself die for something that could not harm me."

"Men have," she whispered. "Countless men, through countless years."

"I could not. I had—I had a thing I wanted to stay alive for."

"Drede?"

He shook his head, said nothing for a long while, his eyes closed, until she thought he was sleeping. And then he straightened, leaned forward and kissed her.

She drew back, her eyes wide, bewildered. "I have never heard of anyone like you. I expected to see you mad or dead in my house, and then find your five brothers at my gates demanding to know why. Instead, you gave Rommalb back his name, and you turn away from death to come back and kiss me on my floor."

"It seemed a better thing to do," he said, smiling, and then the terror of a memory froze the smile on his face, and his eyes emptied, chill as lost stars. He shook it away from him, and rose stiffly. Sybel helped him, her brows quirked worriedly.

"You have such terrible welcomes to my house. I will make Ogam's bed for you. And then I will make Cyrin into sausages."

"No—Sybel, he asked me a riddle, and I asked him for the answer to it. So he gave it to me."

"He tricked me into giving it. And there was no reason for him to treat you this way, a guest in my house, who came out of kindness."

He sat down, then reached after a moment to pick up the pieces of broken bowl. "If you cannot find a reason, I suppose there was none."

"I cannot. Leave that, Coren; I will clean it, after you go to bed."

"No. I will not sleep tonight in darkness. Let me sit here beside your fire. Sybel—"

"What?"

He looked up at her. "Are you afraid of nothing? What are you that Rommalb itself comes obedient to your call?"

"I am afraid of some things. I was afraid for you, then. I am afraid for Tam. But I never thought to be afraid of Rommalb." She knelt to clean the spilled soup, and he watched the firelight pass glittering among the white strands of her hair until they blurred together and he fell asleep.

She found him in the morning still sitting beside the fire, with Gules Lyon at his feet. The snow had stopped; the world was moon-colored beyond the ice-barred windows. A loaf of bread sat half-eaten on the table; the wine was gone. He smiled at her, his eyes red-rimmed, and she said gently,

"You did not sleep well?"

"I woke, and you had gone, so I did not sleep. Cyrin talked with me awhile; he told me tales."

"I hope that is all he told you."

"He told me of Prince Lud, who could have had any flower in the world he wanted, but he wanted only the flaming rose that grew on the Black Peak of Fyrbolg. And he got what he wanted and was content. So I still hope."

Color rose about her eyes. "I do not think any of this is Cyrin's business. Besides, you said yourself I am no flaming rose, but an ice flower, growing in a lifeless world. You belong in the world of the living, and there, I think, you will find your rose."

He sighed. "And you said, sometimes I am a fool. I think I am the one who has been living until now in a lifeless world. Sybel . . . last night I dreamed of Norrel. Always—always before, when I dreamed of him, I never saw him as he was alive, but only as he lay dying, alone, feeling the death wound in him, seeing Drede turn away from him, trying to call, with no voice to call, no one to hear him—I see him call me in my dreams, and he does not see me, and I cannot come to him. But last night, I fell asleep watching you clean the floor, and I dreamed of Norrel as he was alive, when we would talk together late at night. He was talking to me of Rianna, of his love for her. And I was smiling, listening, nodding, because I understood how he felt, what he was saying. I woke, still hearing his voice, and in the moment of my waking, I thought of Drede and I felt pity for him, because he could not have what Norrel had . . . Sybel, he is only an old, frightened man, with no one to love him but Tamlorn. And I thought he was like Rommalb, a death giver . . ."

"Do you still want him dead?"

"I think—I am tired of thinking about him." He rose, came to her, stood before her without touching her. "I love you. When you need me again I will come."

"No, Coren," she said helplessly, and found she had reached out to touch him. "I am not good at loving. In all my life, I have only loved Maelga, Tam and Ogam, even though he was not very good at loving either. Stay in Sirle, where there are women who—who can give you what you require. I belong here."

"I require you," he said simply. He turned to get his cloak. "When the Prince Rurin pursued the witch Glower for turning all his servants into pigs, she—"

"I know. She thrust a great mountain of glass in his path that he could neither ride over or around. So he returned, defeated."

"So," Coren said, and bent to kiss her unresponsive face farewell. "What is the difference between glass and ice?"

"Oh, go home," she said crossly, then laughed in spite of herself. She went to the gates with him to let him out. She stood shivering in the soundless morning, watching him ride down the mountain. The Boar Cyrin came to stand beside her, his warm breath blossoming in and out of the air. She looked down at him.

"That was a great chance you took," she said soberly. The silver-bristled Boar grunted his private note of laughter. He used with her, for the first time, his bell-sweet voice.

"One wise fool knows another."

Tam came to visit her a few days later. She looked up from her reading to hear Ter's voice and see him circling her domed roof. She threw her cloak over her shoulders and hurried out, and he came to rest on her shoulder, just as Tam rode up to her gates with five men behind him. He slipped off his horse and shouted to her, and she saw his heavy, fur-lined cloak trimmed with gold thread and his soft boots and gloves with cuffs of fur. She opened the gates and he flung himself at her, laughing.

"Sybel, Sybel, Sybel—" He hugged her tightly, then whirled away. "Look at my horse. My father chose him for me—storm-gray, velvet-gray—his name is Drede. He was afraid to let me come, but I begged and begged —I cannot stay long, though—"

"Oh, my Tam, I am glad to see you— Come in." She looked into Ter's glittering eyes and asked, *Is he well?*

The King is kind to him.

Tam walked beside her, his footsteps deep in the snow, his face bright. "Sybel, I am so happy to see you. Drede's palace is so big—there are people everywhere — Sybel, they are so courteous to me, because I am Drede's son. And I have such rich clothes. But I miss Gules Lyon and Nyl."

"Is he good to you?"

"Of course. I am his protection against the Sirle Lords."

She glanced at him, startled. He smiled, his eyes clear.

"You have grown a little, I think," she said.

"Drede says I am like you. But Sybel, he is very kind to me, and I am happy; when we are alone together, sometimes, doing simple things—then sometimes he laughs." He opened the door. Moriah came to meet him, purring. He knelt down and rubbed his chilled face along her fur, then reached for Gules Lyon's mane and stared into the golden eyes. "Gules," he whispered, "Gules," and the deep throat rumbled. "Do you know what I miss, too, Sybel? Your green fire. It is so beautiful." He shook snow from his cloak. She touched his pale, wet hair.

"You are growing," she said wonderingly, and he laughed, his voice deepening.

"I know. Sybel, he wanted me to bring you back with me, but I said I would only ask you—I would not beg. I have asked you, and now we can talk about other things. Are the animals well?"

A smile trembled in her eyes. "Very well," she said, and went to sit with him beside the hearth. "Tell me now what you do every day."

"Oh—Sybel, I have never dreamed of so many people! We rode through the city on market day, and the people shouted my father's name—and Sybel, they shouted mine, too—Tamlorn—and I was so surprised that my father laughed at me. I like to see him laugh."

She let his voice run over her in a pleasant stream, soothing, comforting; she sat back, watching him, smiling, half listening. His face, bones forming, firming beneath it, lit and changed as he spoke, laughing, sobering, smiling again a clear, curious smile with a hint of secrecy behind it. Her thoughts melted apart; she let them lay strengthless as she had not done for days, and rested content in the warm green fire, and the white walls, and Tam beside her, long-boned, scratching the space between Moriah's black ears as he talked. Then something rippled, minute, distant, unbidden in the deep part of her mind. Tam touched her and she started.

"You are not listening. Sybel, I brought you a gift—a cloak of white wool with blue flowers woven on it. Drede had some women make it for you." He paused a moment. "What is the matter?"

She shook her head. "Nothing. I am a little tired. A cloak? Tam, thank him for me. Is Ter behaving? I was afraid he might eat someone."

"Oh, no. We go hunting on still days. He is very polite with Drede's falcons, but he will let only me take him. Sybel—"

She did not answer him, feeling again the movement in her mind, faint and swift as the movement of a star through the midnight sky. Her hands tightened slowly on the arms of her chair.

"Sybel," Tam said. His brows flicked together. "Do you hurt somewhere? You should talk to Maelga."

"I will." Her fingers loosened, stretched taut. Her eyes sought the fire, wide, black. "I will," she whispered. Then a knocking sounded at the door and Tam's face changed.

"So soon? But I just came."

She turned swiftly. "Oh, my Tam—not yet, surely—"

"I told you I could not stay long." He stood up, sighing. "Sybel, when times are not so troubled, I will stay longer. I have your cloak in my saddlebag." The knocking sounded again; he raised his voice. "I am coming! Sybel, talk to Maelga about what hurts you. She can cure everything."

"Prince Tamlorn—"

"Coming!" He put his arm around her as they walked across the yard, the guard following after them silently. Ter Falcon came to land again on Tam's shoulder. "Sybel, I will stay longer next time. It—I wish you would come to see me."

"Perhaps I will."

"Please come." He unbuckled his saddlebag, and took out a soft, ivory cloak wound with whorls of blue thread. "This is for you."

She touched it. "Oh, Tam, it is beautiful, so soft—"

"It is lined with ermine." He put it in her arms. Then he kissed her quickly. "Please come. And talk to Maelga."

She smiled. "I will, my Tam. Now, may I say one word to Ter?" Tam stood still a moment, and she looked from his gray, smiling eyes to Ter's blue, piercing gaze.

Ter.

What is it, Ogam's daughter? You are troubled.

Tam watched her, saw her face go still a moment, her eyes black, lightless, piercing back at Ter's.

There is someone calling me to him. Stop him.

FIVE

She went to see Maelga that afternoon. The white doves roosted on Maelga's rafters, and the raven came in and out through an open corner of window. The little house was thick with strange scents; Maelga bent murmuring over her cauldron, the steam of it loosening her white curls, plastering them glistening against her cheekbones. She did not look up as Sybel came in, so Sybel did not speak. She moved restlessly, opening and closing Maelga's books, peering at her jars of nameless things, pacing back and forth in the middle of the room, frowning, until Maelga's murmurings stopped abruptly, and she turned her head.

"My child," she said in wonderment. "I am losing count of Things."

"I am sorry," Sybel said. Something she held, worrying with her fingers, snapped; she stared down at it, unseeing. Maelga dropped her spoon in the cauldron. "My bone—"

"What bone?"

"The forefinger of a wizard's right hand. It took me so many years to find one."

Sybel blinked at the broken pieces in her hand. Then she said, "I will bring you bones, if you wish. I will bring you a grinning skull, if I can find the brain beneath it."

Maelga's eyes focused, sharp beneath her untidy curls. "What is it?"

She put the bone down, and her fingers closed tight on her arms. "I am being called. I do not know who is calling me, but I cannot close my mind to him. I am being searched and called surely and skillfully as I would call an animal. I am angry, but so is a fish angry, caught on a line, and so helpless."

Maelga's hands clasped, her rings sparkling. She sat down slowly in her rocking chair. "I knew it," she said. "I knew you would get into trouble stealing those books."

Sybel stopped midpace. "Do you think it is only that?" she said hopefully. Then she shook her head. "No. There is a more powerful mind than mine at work. That frightens me. If he knows I have his books, he does not have to trouble me so for them. Maelga, I do not know what to do. There is no place to hide. If anyone came to do me harm, my animals would fight for me, but there is no one to fight this."

"Oh, dear," Maelga said. "Oh, my dear." She rocked a little, one hand straying through her curls. Then she stopped. "I can do one thing for you. I will send a raven with his black, searching eyes to peer into wizards' windows."

Sybel nodded. "I have sent Ter looking, too." Then she sighed, covering her eyes with her open hands. "I am a fool. If he can call me, he can call Ter, too—"

"If he knows to call him."

"Yes. He may not know Ter. But who? Who is it? I have seen little wizards in their cold towers with straw pallets and dusty books; I have seen greater ones in lords' courts growing fat and pompous with riches. But I have seen no one that I ever thought to fear. I do not know why I am being called." She stared helplessly at Maelga. "What possible reason could there be? I can do nothing for anyone that strong."

"Is he so strong? Perhaps if you do not answer he will yield."

"Perhaps . . . But Maelga, he has broken into my silence, and I cannot follow his call. I cannot find him anywhere, to put a name to him." She resumed her restless pacing, arms folded, her hair drifting behind her like a white cloak. "I am so angry . . . but anger is of no use, and neither is fear. I do not know what to do —I can only hope he is not so strong he can take my name from me."

"Is there a place you can go away to for a while?"

"Where? I could go beyond the borders of Eldwold, and he could still seek me out, bring me to him." She sat down finally, despairingly, beside the fire. "Oh, Maelga," she whispered, "I do not know what to do. If I only had the Liralen . . . I could fly away to the end of the world . . . to the edge of the stars . . ."

"Do not cry," Maelga said anxiously. "You frighten me when you cry."

"I am not crying. Tears are of no use. There is nothing for me but waiting." She turned her head. "Maelga, if—if one day you cannot find me, and no one knows where I am, will you watch over my animals?"

Maelga rose, her hands splayed in her hair. "Oh, Sybel, it cannot come to that. My raven will find him. Ter will find him, and then I will make him such a thing that will dissolve the bones within his skin."

"No, you must keep his finger bone . . ." She rested her cheek against the stones of the fireplace and stared into the flames, seeing nothing as they danced beneath the black cauldron. She sighed. "I will go and let you work. There is nothing you can do for me, and little I can do for myself. Perhaps Ter will find him before he finds me, and perhaps then I can do something."

She rose. Maelga watched her, the lines of her face puckering into worry.

"My white one, be careful," she whispered.

"I will. I hope the one who is calling me has such a friend to give him that warning."

She woke that night to the nudge in her mind, gentle as a fingertip stirring water. She sat straight in her bed, her eyes wide to the darkness, while above her the stars flung their icy patterns across the crystal dome. The nudge came again, an unbidden, formless thought, and she heard like a whisper in a motionless night, the faint, breathed call of her name.

Sybel.

A small cry broke from her in the darkness. She heard a movement by her bed; Gules' golden eyes sparkled like cut stones.

What is it you fear, Ogam's child?

I had a dream . . .

And the voice came again, a toneless murmur: *Sybel.*

She spent a day and a night in the domed room, neither eating nor sleeping, searching ancient books for the name of such a powerful wizard, but she found no hint of it. At dawn, she let the book fall limp in her hands and stared out at the clearing sky. A line of rose traced the rim of the world; white clouds, silver-rimmed, blazing, caught the sun's rays, broke and scattered them over Fallow Field, over the Plain of Terbrec, across the walled city of Mondor, where they warmed the chill, dark walls and towers. She thought hopelessly of the Liralen with its bright, white wings, and called it a little, sending the call toward the white dawn world. The animals began to stir in the house. Then she heard Maelga's voice, calling at her door.

"Sybel! Sybel, wake up—"

She rose slowly, stiff, and went through the chill house. The sun streaked the snow with fire; it leaped at her eyes as she opened the door, hurting them. She blinked.

"Maelga. Come in."

"Oh, Sybel—you have let your fire die." She stepped in, and Sybel stared at the dark thing in her hands.

"That is not the only dead thing in this room, I think." She touched the black, stiff body of Maelga's raven. A lightning stroke of fear she had never known before shot through her. Maelga said wearily,

"Sybel, I sent him out, and this morning he flew into my house and dropped dead at my feet. I think he was dead as he flew."

Sybel shuddered. "It is cold," she murmured. "I am sorry." She stared down at the motionless bird until Maelga touched her gently, and she started.

"Sybel, you are tired. Have you eaten lately?"

"I do not think so. I have been reading." Her shoulders, strained taut, fell suddenly; she covered her face with her hands. Maelga's arms closed about her.

"My white child," she mourned, "what can I do for you?"

"Nothing," Sybel whispered. "Nothing." She dropped her hands, sighing. "I hope Ter is safe. I will call him, send him back to Tam."

"I will cook you something. You are so thin since Tam left."

She went into the kitchen, still carrying the dead raven. Sybel caught the Falcon's mind, felt the sudden sweep of earth beneath its flying.

Ter. Go back to Tam. There is danger.

There was silence a moment, before the drive of Ter's heartbeat and the run of fire in his veins. Then he said,

No.

Ter. Go back to Tam.

Ogam's child, ask of me anything else. But I have a pair of eyes to pick and a dark mind to still.

Ter—

She lost him suddenly, groped for him, amazed, and lost him again; and a whisper broke into her mind, strong, implacable.

Sybel.

"No," she said, and the word fell lifeless against the white stones. "No!"

She sat under the domed roof at midnight, and the full moon watched her like an eye. The world lay silent beyond the dome, hushed and hidden; the mountain itself was still, the stars frozen like ice crystals. The night was voiceless as her own mind, resting in its heart of silence that no wind, no whisper of leaves disturbed. Her eyes were dark in the darkness, motionless as she waited, listening to the quiet of her mind, waiting for the moment, the calls that rippled to the core of its silence. Gules lay beside her, his head raised, golden eyes unblinking, motionless as though he did not breathe. She felt movement near her after a while and found Cyrin, the gleam of his tusks white as starlight.

Answer me a riddle, Lord of Wisdom, she said to him, and in his mind heard the swift passage of all the riddles of the world. And his red eyes vanished as his great, glowing head sank before her.

That one I cannot answer.

Her head dropped onto her knees. "I am weary," she whispered, wide-eyed, to the darkness. "I do not know what to do." She sat there awhile, still, feeling now and then the faint tug of herself away from herself, like the soft withdrawal of a moon-drawn wave. The moonlight etched her shadow on the white marble floor, and the dark massive shadows of Boar and Lyon. She closed her eyes finally, sent forth a call. And as she called she heard a faint, familiar shouting at her gates.

"Sybel," Coren said, as she ran through the night

snow to him. "Sybel." His hands were closed tight on the bars as though he had tried to pull them apart. "I am sorry—I am so sorry—I was away from Sirle—"

"I just called you," she said breathlessly, pulling at the frozen bolts. "Just a moment ago—Coren, did you fly here?"

"I tried to." He led his horse in, stopped in front of her, trying to see her face in the dark. "What is it?" he said anxiously. "Sybel, I wanted to come three days ago, but Rok had sent me to Hilt to talk to Lord Horst about some hopeless plan— I knew you were troubled; I knew it even while I slept, but I could not leave until yesterday. What is it? Is it Tam?"

She stared up at his shadowed face, wordless. She shook her head. "No. How—how did you know I wanted you before I knew that?"

"I knew. Sybel, what is it? What can I do for you?"

"Just—a little thing."

"Anything."

"Just—hold me."

He dropped the reins in the snow. He opened his cloak, drew her into it until it closed on her white hair, and the crown of her head gleamed faintly below his face. She dropped her head against him, smelled the dark, damp fur around her, felt the draw of Coren's breath and the beat of his blood. His breath caught, and she opened her eyes.

"Sybel—you are afraid."

"Yes."

"But—"

"Hold me closer," she said, and his arms shifted around her, drew her nearer. She heard his heart beneath her ear, felt one gloved hand cupping her head. She drew a long, slow breath and loosed it. "I would have called you all the way from Sirle to ask you to hold me like this. Just for this."

"I would have come. I would have come only to do

this and to go back. But Sybel, there must be more I can do for you."

"No. Your voice is like the sunlight; it belongs to the world of men, not the dark world of wizards."

His voice tangled in her hair. "What is it? What is troubling you?"

She was silent. Then she lifted her head, sighing, drew away from him and the circle of his arms broke. "I did not want to tell you. But now perhaps I should, because if anything happens to me, you—you may be troubled until you know."

His hands rose, creased with snow, to circle her face, and his voice rose. "Sybel—what?"

"Come in to the fire. I will tell you."

She told him after he had stabled his horse in her shed and fed it. He hung up his cloak by the fire and sat beside her. She gave him a cup of heated wine and said simply,

"I am being called."

He stared at her, over the rim of his cup. Then he put it down sharply, and the wine splashed over his fingers. "Who?"

"If I could put a name to him, I could fight him, perhaps. I have looked everywhere for a name to put to him; I have surprised wizards beyond Eldwold with the whisper of my voice in their minds, and their own fear and wonder have told me they do not know me. So now—I do not know what to do. He has taken Ter Falcon; I sent Ter to look for him, and he stole Ter's name from me, and I could not hold Ter against his power. He is very strong. I think he is stronger than anyone I have ever heard of. So, I think, I will have to yield to him."

He was silent, his brows twisted. "I do not think," he said finally, "that I will yield you to him."

She shifted uneasily. "Coren, that is not what I called you for. You cannot help me."

"I could try. I could not—I could not help Norrel, but I will help you. I will stay here with you, and when he comes for you, or when you go to him, I will be there beside you, and he will answer to me."

"Coren, what good would that do? I would only have to watch you die, or watch your mind being twisted against itself so that you could never speak my name again. Rommalb was terrible, but not evil. Rommalb was fear, and you survived that, but this wizard, for you, would be death."

"Then what shall I do?" he demanded helplessly. "Do you think I could sit here, or in Sirle, meek as a child while you are taken by some danger without a name?"

"Well, I will not watch you die in front of me."

"Well, I would rather do that than lie awake at night with your troubled mind tugging at me, and not know where you are, why you are troubled."

"I never asked you to come uncalled when I was troubled. I never asked you to listen for my voice."

"I know: You never asked me to love you. Well, I do love you, and I am troubled, and I will stay with you no matter how much you argue. It is easy to call a man into your house, but not so easy to have him leave."

"You are a true child of Sirle, to think every danger can be frightened away by an unsheathed sword. I thought you were wise, but you are stupid. Did you go to battle at Terbrec against Drede with a spell book in your hands? Well, then what good will it do you to meet a wizard in battle with a sword than can be turned against you with one word? When that wizard melts your sword into a pool at your feet, what will you do next?"

He was wordless, his mouth tight. Then suddenly, he shrugged. "I am stupid to argue with you. Unless you can pick me up and throw me out, Sybel, here I stay. You may ignore me and walk over my feet, and refuse to feed me, but when you go I will follow you, and I will do my best to kill anything that harms you."

She rose. She looked down at him, her black eyes distant, quiet, and as he met her eyes, he heard the faint stirrings about him of waking beasts. "There is a way," she said, "to send you back to Sirle reluctant, but alive."

Gules Lyon, yawning, its eyes of luminous gold, moved soundless as a shadow from the domed room, milled a circle around Coren, brushing restlessly against him. In the kitchen, Moriah, wakened, murmured a deep-throated song that had no words, melted leisurely toward them. Coren, his eyes on the still black eyes, saw them go momentarily lightless, and heard, in the soundless night, the slow pulse of great winds sucking against the air. He straightened, reached out to Sybel, his hand warm on her wrist, and her thoughts came back to him. He met her gaze, held it while the soft snort of Boar and suck of Dragon wing wove a frail web of sound burst by the Cat's sudden, full-throated scream of warning. Then he tugged at her a little, as though shaking her out of a dream.

"Sybel. Are you trying to make me afraid? Why do you not just go into my mind, as you went into Drede's mind, and send me quietly without my knowledge, back to Sirle? I could not argue with that."

She stared at him a moment without answering. Then her face twisted, and she broke away from him. He rose quickly, caught her, and she dropped her face into her hands. "I cannot," she whispered. "I want to, but I cannot."

"Then what? If you set these animals at me, I will fight them, and they will be hurt, and so will I. And then we will both be angry with each other for letting such a thing happen. Sybel, it would be better for both of us, you and I, if you simply let me care about you. Let me keep my foolish watch here—care enough for me to let me do that. It is the only thing I can do. Please. You owe me some kindness."

She dropped her hands. The long fall of her hair hid her face; he could not see it in her silence. Then she shook it back, looked up at him, her eyes quiet, weary with waiting.

"I want you to go. For your sake I would tie you to Gyld and send you to Sirle, to Rok's doorstep. But for my sake, there is no place I want you but here. Will you go?"

"Of course not." He drew her close to him until her head dropped forward onto his breast, and he smiled vaguely at Gules Lyon, his lips brushing the top of her hair. She whispered against him,

"I am selfish. But Coren, this one thing I know, and I will tell you now: where I am going, in the end, I will go alone."

She lay awake that night with Gules Lyon at the foot of her bed, and Moriah at her doorway, and the great, cold worlds of fire splayed silent above her head. She felt the steady pulse of the call in her mind, rippling through the silence, through the opened doors and corridors of it, moving downward, steadily, strongly, to the deep places where she kept the clear, cold knowledge of herself in her ground mind. The call moved inevitably toward that place, while her own powers ebbed away, her thoughts lay useless, unformed in her mind. Finally, there was nothing in her but that call, numbing her will, turning the white still house unfamiliar to her until it seemed the shadow of a dream. The deep, secret places of her mind lay open, unprotected; her power was measured, her name taken, all that her name meant: all experience, all instinct, all thought and power was measured and learned.

She rose at a command that was scarcely more than a word, and dressed so softly that cloth barely whispered against cloth. A great, gold Lyon lay sleeping in the moonlight; a black Cat, nameless, stretched like a shadow across the threshold. She looked at them, found no names in her mind to wake them, for their names lay like jewels in a deep mountain, hidden from her mind's eye. She stepped over the sleeping Cat so gently its eyes did not flicker. In the room beyond, a red-haired man sat before a green flame, his eyes closed, his hands open, limp. She moved past him silent as a breath in the still room, past the silver-bristled Boar asleep at his feet.

The door clicked softly, closing, and Coren started awake. He looked around, blinking. A twig snapped in the fire and he leaned back again, watching the dark room where Sybel slept guarded by Gules and Moriah. And as he watched, Sybel led his horse silently through the snow, out of her gates. She mounted and rode it bareback down the long, fire-white mountain path, past Maelga's sleeping house, down toward the dark, towered city of Mondor.

SIX

She climbed the winding steps of a high tower on the north wall of the city. They spiraled into shadow above her, below her; her own shadow, shaped by torchlight, loomed before her up the worn stones. At the end a light limned a closed door. She gripped the heavy iron ring of its latch and opened it.

"Come in, Sybel."

She walked into a round room. A canopy of woven stars glittered brilliant, motionless above her head; white wool and linen etched with ancient tales in rich threads hung from the walls, breathed gently over the high, thin windows. She stepped on soft sheepskin, ankle-deep, that lay the length of the room. A warm fire glowed in the middle of the room. Before it stood a tall man in a robe of black velvet with a silver belt of linked moons at his hips. He stood silently, watching her. His face was lean, hawk-lined, with no hint of feeling but for a single brief line curving faint beside a corner of his mouth. His eyes were cool, deep-shadowed green.

"Give me your name."

"Sybel."

At the word the invisible thread of the call that had

shadowed her mind broke, and she stood free, blinking in the room. She shivered a little, her eyes moving dark over the walls. The green eyes watched her, unmoved.

"Come to the fire. You have had a cold journey in the snow." He held out his hand, lean-boned, long-fingered, with a single jeweled ring on his forefinger the color of his eyes. "Come," he said again, insistently, and she moved to the firebed slowly, unclasped her wet cloak.

"Who are you? What do you want with me?"

"My name now is Mithran. I have called myself many things through the years. I have served princes in outlandish courts in many worlds; I serve them quietly and well—if they are powerful. If they are not, I use them for my own purposes."

Her eyes moved, black, to his face. "Who do you serve now?" she whispered. The line trembled, gossamer-faint, at the corner of his mouth.

"Until this moment I have been in service. But now, I think I might serve myself."

"Whose service?"

"A man who at once fears you and wants you."

Her lips parted. The breath hissed through them, startled. "Drede?"

"You are surprised. Why? You called him twice from his house, so skillfully he did not know what impulse moved him. He is fighting for his power in Eldwold, and the only weapon he has is his young son against the six sons of Sirle."

"I told him I would not meddle in their affairs! Why does he think I would go against him, the father of Tam?"

"Why not, when a red-haired Sirle lordling courts you with his sweet words? You have raised Tamlorn, but you have your own life to lead. You are powerful and—beautiful as a rich line of poetry from an ancient, jewel-bound book. How can Drede be sure that an impulse will not move you to Coren?"

"Coren—" She covered her eyes with her fingers, feeling them cold. "I told Drede—"

"You are not made of stone."

"No. I am made of ice." She whirled away from the fire, stopped beside a gleaming table, her hands splayed on it. "You know my mind. You know it better than any man alive. I have made difficult choices, but always my own freedom to use my power serving my own desires, harming no one, has been my first choice. Why can he not see that?"

"You loved Tam. Why can you not love Coren of Sirle? You are capable of love. It is a dangerous quality."

"I do not love Coren!"

He stepped away from the fire toward her, his eyes unblinking, unreadable on her face. "And Drede? Do you love him? He would make a queen of you."

Blood rose in her face. She stared unseeing at goblets of moon-colored silver on the table. "I was drawn to him a little . . . But I will not sit meekly beside him, dispensing my power as he sees fit, drawing Sirle to its doom—I will not!"

The calm, sinewy voice pursued her, inflexible. "I am paid to render you to him so meek."

Her hands slipped from the wood. She turned to him, the blood slipping from her face, her eyes narrowed as though she were listening to words of a strange spell. "Drede—wants—"

"He wants you obedient to him. He wants you to know he can love you, trust you without question, as he can trust no one else in the world. He knows you somewhat. And he thinks there is but one way to achieve this. He hired me to do it."

A fear such as she had never known began to stir deep in her, send chill, thin roots through her blood, her mind. "How?" she breathed, and felt tears run swift across her face.

"You know, I think. Sybel. How much that name means to you—memory, knowledge, experience. There is not one possession more truly, irrevocably yours. Drede has hired me to take that name from you for a while, then give it back to another woman, who will smile and accept it, and then give to Drede, without question, forever, what he asks."

A sound came out of her, so sharp and grating she did not recognize her voice. It came again; she slid to her knees on the skins, the hot tears catching between her fingers. She groped for breath, words wrenching from her, "Help me—I am torn out of myself—"

"Have you never wept so before? You are fortunate. It will pass."

She caught the sobbing between her clenched teeth, her hands clenched on the wool. She turned her head, looked up at him, her face glittering in the firelight.

"Let me see him. I will—I will do whatever he wants. Only do not take my will from me. I will marry him. I will walk meekly beside him—only let me choose to do so!"

The green eyes gazed down at her, inscrutable. The wizard moved after a moment, stooped beside her. He touched her face; tears winked like stars on his fingertips.

"I wept so once . . ." he whispered. "Many years ago, even with the ashes of years of loving and hating cold in my heart. I wept at the flight of the Liralen and the knowledge that though I might have power over all the earth that one thing of flawless beauty was lost to me . . . I never thought another thing of such white beauty would fall into my keeping. The King requires that it pass from my hands to his . . . And he such a small man to tame such freedom . . ."

"Will you let me talk to him?"

"How could he trust you? He trusted Rianna once, and she betrayed him in secret. He wants no betrayal this time. He is afraid of you and jealous of Coren. Yet your face burned once under his hand, and the young prince loves you. So he would take you to him —not powerless, but controlled.

"What is he paying you?"

The still eyes lined faintly in a smile. "All this—riches, leisurely hours in luxurious privacy, your animals, if I break the power of the Sirle family forever. I have not yet decided to do that."

"Why is he not afraid of you?" she whispered. "I am."

"Because when he first spoke to me, he had nothing else I wanted. Now, I am not sure of that."

"What else do you want?"

"Do you seek to buy your freedom from me?"

"I cannot buy it from you! You must give it freely, if at all, out of pity."

He shook his head slowly from side to side. "I have no pity. I have only awe of you . . . You have a powerful mind, lonely in its knowledge, for the experience of the mind is secret, unsharable. I have been in wastelands beneath the moon's eye, in rich lords' courts with the sound of pipe and heartbeat of drum . . . I have been in high mountains, in hot, small witches' huts watching their mad eyes and fire-burned faces; I have spoken with the owl and the snow-white falcon and the black crow; I have spoken to the fools that dwell by thousands in crowded cities, men and women; I have spoken to cool-voiced queens. But never in all my wanderings did I dream there existed one such as you . . ." His hand lifted, the ringed finger touching a strand of her hair. She drew back a little, her eyes wide on his face.

"Please. Let me talk to Drede."

"Perhaps . . ." He rose, stepped away from her. "Get

up. Take your wet cloak off and warm yourself. I have hot food and wine. There is a bed for you with rich hangings behind that curtain and something else that belongs to you."

She got up slowly, and drew back the white curtain. Ter Falcon perched on a stand of gold; his glittering eyes stared at her indifferently. She groped for his mind, speaking his name silently, but nothing of him answered her, and he did not move. She turned wearily.

"You are strong, Mithran . . . It is strange that I should be here at your mercy because I chose to love a helpless baby twelve years ago. I am afraid of you and Drede, but fear will not save me, and I do not think anything might save me except you."

The black-robed wizard poured her wine. At the windows, the curtains were growing pale with morning. "I told you, I have no pity. Eat. Then rest awhile, and I will bring Drede to you. Perhaps he has some pity left in him, but a man afraid in the core of his mind has little room for compassion."

Drede came at noon. The draw of the bolt on the door woke Sybel; she heard his low voice.

"Is it done?"

"No."

"I told you I did not wish to speak to her until it was done!"

The wizard's voice came, cold. "I have never done this before. It goes against me. You will flaw her beyond repair; she will be beautiful, docile, powerful only at your command."

"You told her that—"

"Yes. It is nothing. She will forget. But she wished to speak to you—beg you—"

"I will not listen!"

"I have told you: I have turned against myself to do this thing. If I must bear the guilt for it, so must you, or I will not do it."

Drede was silent. Sybel rose and drew back the curtain. The King's eyes leaped to her face; she saw shame in them, torment, and beneath them the icy glaze of fear. She stood still a moment, her hand on the curtain. Then she went to him and knelt at his feet.

"Please," she whispered. "Please. I will do whatever you ask. I will marry you. I will put the Sirle Lords under your power. I will raise Tam, and I will bear you sons. I will never argue with you; I will obey you without question. But do not let him take my will from me. Do not let him change my mind. It is a terrible thing, more terrible than if you killed me here, now. I would rather you do that. There is a part of me, like a white-winged falcon, free, proud, wild, a soaring thing that goes its own way seeking the bright stars and the sun. If you kill that white bird, I will be earthbound, bound in the patterns of men, with no words of my own, no actions of my own. I will take that bird for you, cage it. Only let it live."

Drede lifted one hand, covered his eyes. Then he knelt before Sybel and took her hands in his hands, holding them tightly. "Sybel, I am helpless in this matter. I want you, but I am afraid of you—afraid of that white bird."

"I promise—I promise—"

"No, listen to me. I have been—I have lived afraid always of those I hold in power. I have been threatened by my lords, betrayed by those I loved, until there is no one I can speak the truth to without being afraid. My own people, the ones I should trust, I look into their eyes, their secret, expressionless eyes, and I suspect them, I fear their treachery. I am alone. Tamlorn is the one thing in this world I trust and love. You, I could love, and perhaps trust, but I must be certain of you, Sybel."

She said, her mouth dry, "You—cannot ever be certain of those you love—that they will not hurt you, even loving you. But to make me certain to love you, will be to take away any love I might give you freely. That white bird's name is Sybel. If you kill it, I will die and a ghost will look out of my eyes. Trust me. Let me live, and trust me."

His eyes closed, tightening. "I cannot—I trusted Rianna, and she betrayed me, smiling. She smiled at me, and kissed my palm, and betrayed me for a blue-eyed Sirle lordling. And you—you would marry me, and turn to Coren—"

"No!"

"But how could I be sure? How? One day he would walk smiling into your garden, and you would smile back, and all your promises to me would scatter like leaves on the wind."

"No— You are talking of Rianna, not me— I have nothing to do with Rianna and Norrel! Let me go! Please let me go! I will go back to my white hall, and this wizard can put a wall around it that I will never cross. I will leave Eldwold! I will do anything—anything—"

His words came whispered through his teeth. "Sybel, I dream of you at nights, and I wake alone and weep. It will be done swiftly, and then you will be with Tamlorn—"

"No—"

He loosed her, rising, his hands clenched. "It will be done!"

"So," she whispered, trembling, her eyes dry, unseeing. "I am never to love again. That is harsh, considering that I am the first of three wizards to learn how. I would like to kill myself, but I will not be permitted to make even that small choice. I hope you pay this wizard well, because this deed is without price and without parallel."

He stood a moment wordless before her. Then he turned, and she heard the whisper of his steps across the sheepskin, and then the beat of them down stone steps. The door closed, the bolt shot, and at the sound she gave a frightened, hopeless cry.

"Get up, Sybel."

She rose unsteadily. Mithran went to the table, poured wine. He gave her a cup and sat down, sipping, watching her across the rim of his goblet.

"Sit down."

She sat. She whispered into the cup, "Give me a few minutes of freedom."

"To take yourself out of this world forever? No, you are too valuable."

"Leave one small place for freedom in my mind."

"To love?"

She lifted her eyes. "To hate," she whispered. Her fingers circled the cup, kneading the wrought silver. "In that one small corner I could breed such a hate that would tear Eldwold apart stone by stone, and leave a wasteland for the Sirle Lords to bicker over for centuries. I would bring that King to his knees as he brought me to mine."

The green eyes watched her, unwavering. "And what of me? Do you hate me?"

Her eyes moved lifeless to his face. "You are beneath hatred."

He leaned forward, the ring on his finger flashing darkly. His mouth tightened suddenly. "He is a fool, that King. More so than most men. Did you know that you stole a book from me once?"

She blinked. "No. I would remember you."

"The spell book of the wizard Firnan. You thought the room was empty. A lonely, cold room in a small lord's court near Fyrbolg. I was there. I watched you enter, silently, as though the air had formed you. You looked through my books, took that one, and left so silently . . . and I watched that place in midair for hours after you went. I did not know your name. I did not know even if you belonged to Eldwold. I only knew that you came before me like the answer to a dream that I had not even dared dream . . . So I began to listen, to ask a question here and there, and I began to learn of you . . ."

She stared at him wonderingly. "But why did you call me for Drede?"

"It is he who told me at last who to call. You see, I am no fool. If I had come to you in your mountain house, you could have said yes to me as easily as no. Today, though, I think there is only one answer you will give me. I want you. If I must take you by force, I will, though with such a choice that you face today, I doubt that you will argue. I am powerful; my knowledge is inexhaustible. I have both loved and hated, but for years I have found nothing worth either loving or hating until I saw you. I can share thoughts, experiences with you as I can with no one else. I loved a woman once for her beauty. I never thought I might want to again. It is as though—as though you were made for me."

She stared at him numbly. She began to tremble again; she held herself, her fingers tight, cold on her arms. He said,

"Drink."

She drank wine. She leaned forward, dropped her head on her arms. Mithran watched her, motionless.

"Well?"

"This is my fault, a little," she whispered. "Maelga warned me."

"Look at me."

She raised her head, her eyes wide, mute on his face. His thin brows flickered a little, drawing together. "Does it require such thought?"

"I am not even thinking. There is only emptiness."

"Sybel. Choose."

"I do not care. I do not care! You choose! If you

want me, then keep me—if not, give me to Drede. What do you want me to do? Thank you for giving me a place in the wasteland of your heart? Drede at least I understand, but you—you are colder than I am."

"Am I so?" he breathed. He checked himself, his thin mouth tightening again at the corners. "White bird, you know I will never give you to that King. Nor will I break your mind to suit either him or me."

"You have already broken it!" she cried. "White bird—white falcon on a silver thread, to come when you call— I would fear you until I died, you have such power over my slightest thought. So I do not care now what you do to me. Do you want me to beg you to save me from Drede? I will go down on my knees to you for that, but I can never give you thanks for it if I am shackled to you."

"You could not—try to love me?"

"I love no one! I will never love anyone! So Drede will have me helpless and smiling, or you will have me helpless and afraid—which do you prefer?"

He sat silently a moment, a finger moving up and down his cup, while she watched him, her hands tight on the arms of her chair. He said softly, his words measured to the slow movement of his hand, "You will not always fear me, Sybel. I will show you ancient arts and spells even you have never dreamed of learning. I will give you wondrous things: the purple jewel the shape of an eye made by the witch woman Catha that sees into locked doors and boxes; the cloak made of the skins of the blue mountain cats of Lomar, soft as the whisper of breath, warm as the touch of a mouth . . . I will give you the locked, bound books of the wizard Erden, never opened since his death three centuries ago, and I will tell you how to open them . . ." His words formed like dreams in her mind; she felt herself lulled, her mind eased, darkened. "I will capture for you the winged gazelle of the Southern Deserts, with eyes like the luminous night . . . You will sleep in white wool and purple silk, and wear jewels the color of stars with red and blue fire in their midst . . ." As from far away she saw him rise slowly, shadow-silent, come toward her, his voice low, weaving visions for her that formed and rested in her numbed mind. She felt his fingers straying through her hair. "I will give you the silver-stringed harp of the Lord Thrace of Tol, that plays at command, sings lost tales of dead, glorious kings . . ." His breath whispered against her face. A cry rose in her somewhere, faint as a child's cry in the night that faded, lost. She felt his hands at her throat, saw the silver circle of her brooch wink and tremble in the light. "I will give you the Cup of Fortune that was thrown by the Prince Verne into the Lost Lake because it foretold his death by water . . ." She felt cloth gathered, tense, in his fingers, heard the hiss of it, torn. She heard the breath shake, faintly between his lips. "I will give you all the treasures of the world, and all its secrets . . . Sybel, my white bird . . ." His head dropped. His lips touched her throat, brushed downward. And then she felt that in his quickening lust for one brief moment he lost her, and she whispered one word without hope, almost without thought.

His head jerked upward, his eyes blazing into hers. He whirled away from her abruptly, and found as he turned the crystal-eyed Blammor behind him. He screamed once, and then the Blammor overwhelmed him like a mist that held him upright an instant, his arms outspread, fingers taut. Then he dropped. The Blammor said to Sybel,

Is there more?

She stared, trembling, at the wizard. Her hands fumbled at her robe, drawing the torn cloth together. *No,* she said. *No more.* And it faded. Beside the bed the Falcon Ter gave a fierce cry of rage. The wizard

Mithran lay on his back, the bones crushed and broken in his face, his hands, his throat. Ter swooped downward, clung to the broken head, his talons piercing the open eyes.

"Ter," Sybel breathed, and he came to her, perched on her chair. She stood, still trembling, and drew on her cloak. Ter's voice floated into her mind; she felt him in his hot rage.

And Drede.

No.

Drede.

No. She went to the door, pulled the bolt with shaking hands. *Drede is mine.*

SEVEN

She rode home slowly through the snow, the Falcon circling above her head, sometimes soaring to heights where he looked to her like a faint dark star in the day sky, then dropping down to her, lightning swift. She spoke to no one, her eyes black, blind, and no one she passed stopped her. She reached the mountain path at twilight. Evening lay silvery against the snow; stars began their slow ascent over the great, dark head of Eld Mountain. The trees were motionless around her, stars caught in their snowy branches. Maelga's house smoked small in the trees, its windows fire-bright. She rode to the yard. As she dismounted Maelga opened the door, stars flaming from her ringed fingers.

"Sybel," she whispered. Sybel stared at her. Maelga came to her, sharp eyes peering, probing. She touched the still, white face. "Is it you?"

"The wizard is dead."

"Dead! How? How, child? I never thought to see you again."

"Rommalb."

Maelga's hand went to her mouth. "You have taken that one, too?"

"Yes. And now the wizard Mithran lies crushed on the floor of his tower, and I think—I think not even his finger bone is whole."

"Sybel—"

She shuddered suddenly, violently. "Let me come in. I need a place—a place to rest awhile."

Maelga's arm closed about her, drew her inside the warm house. Sybel sank down beside the fire, her eyes closing in weariness. She felt hands at the throat of her cloak and started.

"No—"

Maelga's hands checked. She drew a slow breath. Then her fingers brushed lightly down Sybel's cheek and she rose. Sybel untied her cloak, pushed it away from her.

"He tore my dress. Is Coren still at my house?"

"I will mend it for you. Coren is there. He came to me when he found you gone. He blamed himself for sleeping."

"I am so glad he was asleep." She was silent for a long time, staring into the fire. Maelga watched her, rocking silently while the night darkened around the house, and Sybel's face grew shadowed beside the fire. Then Maelga said softly,

"Sybel, what are you thinking? What dark things?"

Sybel stirred. "Night dark," she whispered. Then they heard footsteps in the yard, and the whinny of Coren's horse. Sybel rose, the cloth parting over her white breasts. She opened the door, and Coren, one hand on the back of his horse, looked up to see her framed in the light. He went to her, drew her beneath his cloak, held her, his face hidden against her hair until she felt his tears against her cheek.

"I cried, too," she whispered. "It hurt."

"Sybel, you went from me like a dream, so silently, so irrevocably—I could not bear it, I could not bear it—"

"I am safe."

"But how, Sybel? Who was it?"

"Come in. I will tell you."

He sat with her beside Maelga's fire, his fingers linked hard in hers as though he would never let her go. Maelga, moving softly as she heated a stew for them, cut bread, listened to Sybel's quiet telling.

"It was the wizard Mithran. Have you heard his name?" she asked Coren, and he shook his head. "He saw me once long ago, when I stole a book from him. He—wanted me. He gave me no choice. I asked him for pity, but he had none. He had a very great mind, but it was without challenge, wearied with boredom, bitter deeds. I would have gone with him. I could never have fought him. I would always have been afraid of him. But he made a mistake. He forgot Rommalb. And that was the one name I remembered, when he lost control of himself and me. So he died there."

"I am glad."

"I am, too, except . . . he carried such great knowledge. I wish—I wish we had not met under such circumstances. He was more powerful even than Heald, and he might have taught me things."

Coren stirred beside her. "You do not need such great power to keep your animals. What would you use it for?"

"Power breeds itself. I cannot stop wanting to know, to learn. But I could never have wanted to go with him. He—he did not love me."

"It matters to you, then?"

"Yes." She turned her head to meet his eyes. "It matters."

She heard the long, shuddering draw of his breath. "I wanted to come to you, but I did not know where," he whispered. "Even the snow had fallen to cover your path. I woke, and the fire was dead, and you were gone."

"Coren, there is nothing you could have done for me. He would have had no mercy for you—he had none for me—and I would have had to watch. Then, there would have been no one to hold me when I returned."

"Sybel—" He paused, choosing words. "You have my love. I would have given you my life. And now, I will give up for you another thing: all the weary years of my bitterness toward Drede. If you come with me to Sirle, no one will ever ask anything of you that you do not want to give. I never again want to feel your need of me and not know how to find you. I never want to wake again and find you gone."

She was silent, looking at him, and for a moment he saw in her eyes a shadow of aloofness, of secrecy. Then it passed, and she lifted his hand to her mouth. "And I," she whispered, "do not want to watch you ride to Sirle again without me."

She left Eld Mountain with him the next morning to marry him in his family's house. The long winter was melting to an end: they rode fur-cloaked beneath a sky brilliant with sunlight against the white snow. The Falcon Ter flew above them, black-winged against the sun. They rode past Mondor, across the wide Plain of Terbrec, and then through the forest lands of Sirle, where they spent one night in an outlying farm that was half fortress, the vanguard of Sirle. On the second morning they came to the heartlands of Sirle, the fields, the curve of the Slinoon River, and saw far away the walls and gray stone towers of the home of the Sirle Lords, smoke drifting from its chimneys. They stopped awhile to rest, dismounting. Coren took Sybel's face between his gloved hands, looked into her black eyes.

"Are you happy?" he asked, and his joy bloomed like a flower to her smile. He kissed her eyes closed, murmuring, "Blacker than the fire-white jewel of King

Pwill: the eye in the pommel of his sword that turned black at his death—"

"Coren!"

He loosed her, laughing. The fiery snow winked to the edge of the world; nothing moved in it but the breaths of their horses and the slow smoke of the far Sirle house. Sybel gazed at it, her eyes narrowed a little against the light.

"That will be my home . . . It will be strange, living on flat land, and among people. I am not used to people. It is such a great, gray house. What are in the towers along the wall?"

"Guardrooms, supplies, weapons in case of attack, siege. The Sirle family has never lived quietly among its neighbors. But we were humbled at Terbrec, and now we talk a good deal and do little."

"What are your brothers like? Are they all like you?"

"How, like me?"

"Gentle, kind, wise . . ."

"Am I those things?" he said wonderingly. "I have killed, I have hated, I have lain awake at nights dreaming bitter dreams . . ."

"I have seen great evil, and there is none of it in you." She smiled up at him, but the words shook, in spite of herself, on her mouth. He touched her hair beneath her hood, smoothing it.

"Behind the ancient, thick walls of Rok's house not even a king could find you against your will. Come. My brothers are rough-voiced, battle-scarred, impulsive and foolish, like me, but there is joy in their houses, and they will welcome you simply because I love you."

They rode slowly through the hard, dormant fields, where patches of black, plowed earth thrust upward against the melting snow. They followed a road that wound along the Slinoon River, leading to the threshold of the Lord of Sirle. A young boy with a bow in the empty fields saw them coming: he shouted something that hung in a flash of white breath in the air. And then he ran before them toward the house, the hood bouncing back from his black hair.

"That was Arn," Coren said. "Ceneth's son."

"Are there many children?"

He nodded. "Ceneth has two small daughters, too. Rok's oldest son, Don, is fifteen, a bloodthirsty boy, restless for his first battle. Rok has four younger children. Eorth's wife just had their first son, Eorthling. Herne and Bor have their homes and families in the northern parts of Sirle. And we will have children, you and I, little wizardlings to fill that house."

She nodded absently. Ahead of them, through the open gates, she saw people moving across the snow-patched ground. Water from the Slinoon, trained out of its course, flowed in front of the gates, out toward the fields. In the yard beyond, horses stood saddled, waiting; fire from a smithy within the walls billowed suddenly, died. Arn ran across the drawbridge, vanished within the walls. A few minutes later a man followed him out, stood watching them come.

"Rok."

They joined him at the bridge. He caught Coren's reins, looking up at Sybel, and Coren dismounted. He was a big man, broad-shouldered, with a mane of pale gold hair and a line-scarred face imperturbable as his eyes. His voice, coming out of the deep well of his chest, was unexpectedly mild.

"I expected you home from Hilt four days ago. I was beginning to worry. But now, I see I did not have to." He moved to Sybel's side, took her hand. "You are Sybel."

"How do you know?"

"Because we fought at Terbrec for a woman with a face like yours. You are very welcome to Sirle."

She smiled, looking down into his eyes, seeing in

them despite their calmness a faint, hot edge of triumph. "And you, as Coren says, are the Lion of Sirle. I am grateful for your kind welcome, since I have come so unexpectedly."

"I have learned to expect unexpected things from Coren."

"Rok," Coren said quietly. "We have come to be married here. Sybel has come here as my wife."

Rok's eyes fell, hidden a moment, then lifted again, gold-brown, smiling. "I see. How did you talk her into that?"

"It was not very easy. But I had to do it." He lifted his arms, swung Sybel to the ground. Arn returned to take their horses, staring curiously at Sybel. A tall, red-haired woman followed him out, her thick braids twined among the rich green-and-gold folds of her dress. Coren said, "Lynette, this is—"

"I know, I know." She hugged him, laughing. "Do you think I do not recognize that ivory hair or those eyes? This is Sybel, and you are going to be married. So this is what you have been plotting while we were worrying."

"I do not know why you were worrying. Sybel, this is Rok's wife, Lynette."

"Going off to some place to daydream is one thing," Lynette said, dropping a kiss on Sybel's cheek. "But going to Hilt and not coming back is quite another. Sybel, you look very tired. It must be hard journeying in this cold."

Coren slipped an arm around her. She leaned against him, thoughtless a moment, the fur on his cloak cold, smooth against her face, while he said, "She has been troubled, these past days. Is there a quiet corner in this house where she can rest?"

Sybel straightened. "No, Coren, it is good to hear so many pleasant voices. And I have not met all your brothers or the children."

Lynette laughed. "You will. Come. You can rest in my room, while chambers are prepared for you and Coren."

They crossed the bridge, Arn following behind with the horses, and the bustle in the outer yard stopped while they passed. A smaller gateway led to the inner yard, a square court with trees standing leafless, etching a fretwork of shadows on the snow. A man opened the double doors of the hall, came down the steps to them. His hair was vivid black against the sky; his eyes laughed at Coren, green as stones.

"Arn came babbling of your return, so I thought perhaps you had disturbed some mysterious wizard in your wanderings who sent you home with two heads."

"See how they laugh at me," Coren said to Sybel. "No, Ceneth. The wizard herself came home with me. Now you will have some respect for my comings and goings."

"So. You are the wizard woman of Eld Mountain." His bright eyes appraised her, smiling, speculative, like Rok's. "We have heard much of you from Coren. He has not stopped talking about you since he came home scarred from battle with your dragon."

"If it had not been for Gyld, she would never have let me across her threshold," Coren said. "Where is Eorth? Are Herne and Bor here?"

"They are hunting," Rok said. "They should be back soon." He started at a rush of air above his head, and the Falcon Ter came to rest on Coren's shoulder, surveying them with aloof, brilliant eyes. "Whose is that? It is not one of our hawks—it is huge."

"It is Ter," Coren murmured, turning his head. "He killed seven men . . . What is he thinking, Sybel? I want to know."

"Seven—" Ceneth stared, incredulous, at Sybel. "Is he yours?"

She nodded. "My father, Ogam, called him."

"Is he free?"

"I gave him to Tam, but he still answers to my call when I need him." She was silent, opening her mind to the Falcon, and Rok and Ceneth watched her, motionless. Her eyes came back to Coren.

"He brought me some news of Tam. He is well. I will have to write and tell him where I am. It will be hard for him to understand. I think a part of him still believes Eld Mountain is his true home."

"I doubt if you will have to write," Rok said. "News travels very quickly in Eldwold."

"Does it? It traveled very slowly to me, in my white house. I will write to Tam, anyway; he should hear this from me."

"He will be all right," Coren said gently.

"I hope so."

Ter fluttered off Coren's shoulder, perched to wait on one of the bare trees, and they moved indoors, into Rok's great hall, with skins and pine boughs on the cold stones, ancient tapestry flung across the walls, and a vast hearth where children were playing, rolling on the floor with a hound. Sybel untied her cloak, shook her long hair free, and the children, checked, watched it settle, glistening silver. She found Coren's eyes on her, stranger's eyes, seeing her as though for the first time. She looked away from him, and the blood leaped suddenly through her. Lynette took their cloaks. Coren touched her face briefly.

"Go with Lynette. I will join you soon."

She followed Lynette up a stone stairway beyond the hall, into a wide, bright room. A warm fire snapped on the hearth; two little girls with Lynette's hair lay in front of it, chattering. A baby wailed in a cradle; Lynette caught it up in one arm, and flung aside the hangings around a bed.

"Lara, Marnya, go and play outside. Sh, little Byrd.

Sybel, lie down, if you want to. I will send for food and wine."

Sybel sat down on the bed. "Thank you. I am tired." She rose again a moment later, restlessly, and went to a window. In the distance, beyond the Sirle Forests, she could see the blue-white peak of Eld Mountain glistening against the sky, and knew that far cape of snow curled about a white hall with strange, wondrous animals. Lynette said behind her,

"I know. I felt sad, too, so long ago, leaving my own home in South Hilt. I hope you will be content here. I am glad, for Coren's sake, you came, though I never expected it, not when you gave Tam to Drede."

"I had to. He wanted his father."

"I understand. People like Eorth and Herne have thick heads—they could never understand how you could give a child given to you by Sirle to Drede. To them the whole world is divided by those two names." She propped the quieting baby on her shoulder. Then she smiled at something in Sybel's eyes. "Do you want to hold her? She is my youngest."

Sybel smiled. "You knew my wanting before I did. Coren does that, too." She took the baby, sat down in a chair beside the fire. Gold-brown eyes stared up at her, wary. "Tam was so tiny once . . . And I was so ignorant. Coren says there will be a ceremony, a witnessing, today. What will I have to do?"

"Nothing. Just appear beautiful and ready before the Lord of Sirle, his brothers and their wives and children; Rok will join you, and we will have a feast afterward to celebrate. Did you bring something to marry in?"

"No. I have so few things. I never wanted anything special before."

Lynette eyed her curiously. "You live so simply. Are you going to write to Lord Horst of Hilt to tell him you are marrying Coren?"

"Why?"

"He is your grandfather," Lynette said patiently. "You and Rianna were kin; his daughter was your mother."

Sybel's brows rose thoughtfully. "So. But I doubt if he would care for my kinship, since Ogam called my mother to him the same way he called Ter of Gules. But that is something to remember." She caught Lynette's startled look and smiled. "I did not have a gentle upbringing, like Rianna. If I say anything that disturbs you, tell me. I have known very few people. I did not expect to enjoy them so much as I have today."

Lynette nodded. "I will," she promised. "When I first saw you, I thought of Rianna, and I felt a wrench at my heart, remembering Norrel. But now I think you are something quite different from Rianna. Her eyes were shy and sweet, and yours are . . ." She stared vaguely into them, searching for a word. Sybel shifted.

"Coren says they are black as Drede's heart."

Lynette blinked. "Coren says such things? Why do you marry him, then?"

"I do not know. Perhaps because I could not think of anything else I would rather do."

Lynette nodded, her eyes smiling. She took Byrd, laid her back down in the cradle. "I will go down and see that your things are brought up."

She left. Sybel rose after a moment in the silence, poured herself wine. She leaned over the cradle, touched Byrd's cheek with one finger. Then she turned, pacing restlessly, listening for Coren's step. She heard voices in the yard below, boys' voices, shouting, echoing off the stones in some part of the house. She wandered into the hall, cup in hand and heard, from somewhere within the silent stones, Coren's voice saying,

"No."

She went toward it. Down the corridor, a door stood open; she heard the murmur of men's voices. She stopped at the doorway, her eyes brushing over the long room, searching for Coren. She found him near the fire at the other end. Then slowly, as they spoke, she put names to the five men around him.

"Coren, she is here. Why else would you have brought her here, if not for this?" A slow-voiced man, taller than them all, his hair bright gold, his eyes green as Gyld's wings, asked plaintively. Coren, his voice edged slightly, yet patient, said,

"Eorth, because I love her. Think of her as any other woman here—"

"But she is not as any other woman here," Ceneth said. "Do you think she would be content being treated as such? She has powers; she must use them. Why not for us?"

"Against Drede? I have told you. And I have told you. She wants no war against Tamlorn."

"So? We can put Tamlorn on the throne of Eldwold as easily as Drede can."

"With that woman," a square, weathered man with taut silver hair said, "we can gain support from Hilt—even from Niccon. No one would dare oppose us."

"Bor. No."

"Coren," Rok said, "you went there in autumn for this very thing; to persuade her to come here. You have done it—"

"Not for this! Rok, two days ago, I almost lost her; she was called, harassed by some powerful wizard, and I thought I would never see her again. When she came back, I swore that if she came here, no one would trouble her, try to use her against her will."

"Coren, no one wants to use her against her will. We do not want to make her unhappy here," Bor said. "But surely you can speak to her—not right away, but eventually, when you are easy with each other, settled—"

"I thought that was what you wanted most in life." A small, wiry man looked back at Coren out of his own blue, glittering eyes. "Revenge for Norrel's death."

There was a short silence. Coren, his face taut under his blazing hair, said, "I thought so, too. But now I would rather spend the energy of my thoughts on the living. I gave up everything for her—including my hate. I had to. I cannot explain that to you. Many strange things have happened to me in that white house of hers, and the strangest is that now I would rather think about Sybel than Norrel. If you must war against Drede, you will have to do it without Sybel. This I promised her. If you cannot do it, then you will drive us both out of this house."

There was a murmur of dissent. Rok's hand dropped briefly on Coren's shoulder. "Do not think so little of us. We are all restless, hungry lions—if you toss us a scrap of hope, we will tear it apart with talking. We will not trouble Sybel, if that is how she feels, though you must know how great the temptation is."

"I know. I know."

Ceneth added, "And she will serve great purpose, if only to brighten our house and alarm Drede."

Coren nodded. He glanced around at the silent ring of faces. "I should not trust any of you. But I do. I must. Wait until you see her, Eorth, Herne—you will understand how I could promise such a thing."

"I never will," Eorth said simply. "But if you say she will not help us, then she will not. I can understand that much."

"The wonder of it is that she agreed to marry you at all," Ceneth said, "since she feels that way about Tamlorn and Drede. She must have great courage—or great love—to come into this lions' den with no one but you to protect her."

Coren smiled wryly. "She is very capable of taking care of herself. You have seen Ter Falcon."

"If she can call a Falcon who killed seven men," Eorth said, "surely she can call Drede. Then we could—"

"Eorth," Bor grunted. "Be quiet."

Sybel turned away softly. She went back to Lynette's room, where she found Lynette, her clothes, a tray of food, and five children to watch her eat.

Rok married them that evening in the hall lit with candles held by the children of the sons of Sirle. In the semidarkness the fire billowed and crackled, the only sound in the great room besides Rok's deep, polished voice. Sybel, dressed in flame-red, her hair coiled and braided into a crown of silver by Lynette, stood beside Coren, watching the firelight catch in the strands of gold in Rok's hair, twine through the gold chain on his breast. Rok's voice mingled like a deep forest wind with the breath of the fire; and as he spoke, Sybel's thoughts melted backward to Maelga's house where she had stood in front of Maelga's fire two nights before, her hand in Coren's, in the great heart of the mountain's silence, listening to an ancient binding Maelga spoke, her ringed hands on their hands:

"This bond I draw between you: that though you are parted in mind or in body, there will be a call in the core of you, one to the other, that nothing, no one else will answer to. By the secrets of earth and water, this bond is woven, unbreakable, irrevocable; by the law that created fire and wind this call is set in you, in life and beyond life . . ."

And later that night, before they had left for Sirle, she had lain beside Coren watching the scattering of stars burn beyond the domed roof, listening to Coren's breathing. And curved against him, she had felt the day's darkness drain out of her, felt the weariness deep in her bones flow away. Finally she had slept, deeply, dreamlessly.

"Now," Rok said. "Give your names to each other."

"Coren."

She looked up at him and saw in the red-gold wash

that lit his face a deep flame of laughter that had not been there before in his eyes. She smiled slowly, as though she were accepting the challenge of it.

"Sybel."

EIGHT

When the snow had melted from the warming earth, Rok spoke of building a garden at Sirle for Sybel's animals. She drew plans for him one morning, pictures of Gyld's cave, of the Black Swan's lake, of the white marble hall itself with its great dome, and Ceneth's son, Rok's daughters crowded around her, listening to the tales of them.

"Gyld requires darkness and silence; the Swan of course must have water. Gules Lyon and Moriah must have a walled place, warm in winter, where they will not frighten people and animals. I do not know how they will like being around people—they have all been hunted by men, especially Cyrin. In the Mountain they were secluded. But I cannot leave them alone there, prey to men and to their own impulses. You know how Coren was hurt by Gyld. That may happen easily again to someone less forgiving, and that would be dangerous, both for men and animals. Men may try to trap them, or kill them. I do not want them troubled."

"You care much for them," Rok murmured and she nodded.

"So you would, if you could speak with them. They are all powerful, lordly, experienced. I am very grateful for your help, Rok, and for letting them come here. I hoped for it, but I did not expect it."

"It is a collection worthy of a king's dream," he said, his gold-brown eyes regarding her equivocally. "I am not so loath to make Drede a little afraid."

Her eyes dropped. "I did not think so," she said softly, and he shifted.

"But we will not speak of such matters. There is a large, walled garden between the inner and outer walls that has run wild since the death of our mother. It was built as a place of quiet for her, away from her noisy sons. It has an inner gate, and an outer one beside the keep, opening to the fields. The children rarely play there; our wives have smaller private gardens. It will hold a small lake, many trees, a cave and a fountain for the dragon, but I do not know how to build a crystal dome for you."

She laughed. "If you can do all that for me, I will not ask for a crystal dome. I only need a place for my books, and those I can store in a room. They are very valuable. I should go back to Eld Mountain soon to get them, but I am so comfortable here it is hard to think of a journey."

"I am glad you are happy here." He was silent a moment, while Lara climbed on the back of his chair. "Truthfully, I never expected to see you here. I knew how you felt about Tamlorn, and how Coren felt about Drede; I did not think you could reconcile your loves and hates."

She glanced at him, sketching idly in the margin of her paper. "I have no great love for Drede. Only he is more use to Tam alive than dead. And Coren—I know he has reconciled himself to Norrel's death. But I know, too, he is a man of Sirle, and if you began another war he would fight, not against Drede, but for his brothers, as he fought for Norrel."

"But though we plot and scheme, I see no prospect

of war. No doubt you and Coren will lead peaceful lives in Sirle, at least while Drede is alive."

Her pen stilled. "And then what?"

Rok rose, moving to the fire, with Lara clinging to one powerful leg. "If he dies while Tam is young there will be enough scavengers lying in wait for that young boy's kingdom," he said bluntly. "This is not a quiet world you came down to; Tam must be learning that now, too. If he is shrewd, he may be able to learn to juggle power, giving and taking it. Drede will teach him, so he will not be helpless when Sirle begins to nibble at his kingdom one day."

Her black eyes were lowered, hidden from him. "You are indeed a house of restless lions . . ."

"Yes, but we cannot spring; we have no support, we exhausted arms and men at Terbrec, and we are crippled by the memory." He smiled, disengaging Lara and lifting her to his shoulder, where she sat clinging to his hair. "But this is not something I should be talking about with you. I am sorry."

"There is no need to be sorry. I am interested."

The door to Rok's chamber opened, and Coren looked in. His eyes flicked between their faces.

"What are you doing with my brother?" he asked Sybel wistfully. "You are tired of me. You hate my red hair. You want someone old, gnarled, lined—"

"Coren, Rok is going to build me a garden. Look, we have been drawing plans. This is Gyld's cave, this is the swan lake—"

"And this is the Liralen," he said, touching the graceful lines of her sketch. "Where will you keep that?"

"What is a Liralen?" Rok asked.

"A beautiful white bird, whose wings trail behind it like a wake in the sky. Very few people have ever caught it. Prince Neth did, just before he died. What is it?" he said to Sybel, whose brows had drawn in a vague frown.

"Something Mithran said about the Liralen. He said—he said once he had wept, like I wept that day, because he knew that he could never have power over it, even though he might have power over anything else . . . I wonder how he knew; I wonder why he could not take it."

"Perhaps the Liralen was more powerful than he was."

"But how? It is an animal, like Gules, like Cyrin—"

"Perhaps it is more like Rommalb."

"Even Rommalb can be called."

Coren shook his head, running his fingers down her long hair. "I think Rommalb goes where it wills, when it wills. It chose to come to you, to be bound to you, because it looked into the bottom of the black wells of your eyes and saw nothing there of fear."

"What is Rommalb?" Rok asked. "We have made no plans for it."

Coren smiled. He sat down on the table, pulled the plans toward him. Rommalb is a Thing I met on Sybel's hearth one day. I do not think you would care for it at Sirle. It goes its own way, mostly at night."

Rok's brows lifted. "I am beginning to think some of the tales you have been telling us for nearly thirty years may be true."

"I have always told you the truth," Coren said simply. He laughed at Rok's expression. "There are more dangerous things in Eldwold than troublesome kings."

"Are there? I am too old to meet anything more troublesome than Drede."

"Coren," Sybel said, "I should go to Eld Mountain for my books."

"I know. I have been thinking about that, too. We can leave tomorrow if you want, make a slow journey in this beautiful season."

Rok's voice rumbled in his throat. "It may be dangerous. If Drede does not trust Sybel, he may be lying in wait for her at Eld, expecting her to return for her animals."

"I do not have to go for them," Sybel said. "They can come themselves, when there is a place for them here. But I must have the books."

"I could send Eorth and Herne for them."

She shook her head, smiling. "No, Rok, I want to see my house again, my animals. I will call Ter, and he can spy for us. If there is any danger, he will warn us."

They left for Eld Mountain at midmorning the next day. The winds came cold from the icy peak of Eld, raced across the unbroken plain of the bright sky. The trees in the inner yard were beaded with the hard, dark buds of new leaves. Rok and Eorth went out to watch them leave, their great cloaks billowing like sails in the wind. Eorth said in his slow, deep voice, holding Sybel's stirrup as she mounted,

"Ceneth and I could go with you, Coren. It may be wise."

"I," Coren said, "would like a few days of peace and privacy with a white-haired wizard woman. Do not worry about us. Sybel will transfix with one eye anyone who dares accost us." He turned his horse, one hand raised in farewell, and like a bolt out of the blue sky Ter landed on his arm. Rok laughed.

"There is your guard."

Coren grimaced at the taut, heavy grip. "Go sit on Sybel; I will guard myself." He glanced at Sybel and fell still, seeing the look pass from woman to bird like a bond. Sybel gave a murmur of surprise.

"What is it?"

"Tam. He left Mondor this morning for Eld Mountain. I wonder that Drede let him go. Unless—"

"Unless," Rok said, "Drede knows nothing of his

leaving. Extend an invitation of our hospitality to Tam, if you see him."

"We had him once," Coren said briefly. "And we lost him. Let it be."

Rok smiled. "I am sure Drede has trained him well. Besides, when you reach the Mountain, he will no doubt be on his way home again. Go. Enjoy your journey. Send Ter to us if you need help."

They rode slowly across Sirle, through the forest land, spending the night in a tiny farmhouse on the very edge of the Plain of Terbrec. They reached Eld Mountain in the early afternoon of the next day. The winding road was damp with melted snow; the Mountain blazed against the blue sky; winds, tangy with the scents of snow and pine, tasted like some rare wine. Sybel drew back her hood, let her hair stream like white fire in the wind; the brush of its chill drew blood beneath her clear skin. Coren caught her hair, wound it through his fingers, drew her head back and kissed her, and sunlight splashed hot on her closed eyes. They rode to the white hall and found the gate unlocked.

Tam came out to meet them.

He walked slowly, Gules Lyon at his side, his eyes wide, uncertain on Sybel's face. She slipped from her horse with a startled exclamation.

"Tam!" She went to him, took his face between her hands. "My Tam, you are troubled. What is it? Has Drede—has he done something?"

He shook his head. Her hands dropped tight to his shoulders. "Then what?" His face was winter-pale, smudged; his eyes rimmed with sleeplessness. He put his hands on her arms, then looked past her to Coren, who had dismounted to take Sybel's horse.

"Is he angry with Drede?"

Her fingers tightened. She said quickly, startled. "He knows nothing. But you, Tam, what have you learned? How?"

He shook his pale head wearily. "I do not understand anything. Drede said you were going to marry him, and I was happy, and then he—suddenly something frightened him, and he would not speak of you; and when I told him you had married Coren, his face went so white I thought he would faint. But I touched him, and he spoke, and—he is so frightened it hurts me to see him. So I came to you to see if—what he was frightened of. I knew you would come, if Ter told you I was here."

"Tam, does he know you are here?"

"No. No one does." He looked over her shoulder as Coren came to them and said stiffly, "I see one of the seven of Sirle. I am taught to fear you."

Coren said gently, "Ter sits on my shoulder and takes meat from my fingers, leaving the fingers behind. To him I am only Coren who loves Sybel."

Tam's hands dropped from Sybel's arms. He sighed, his face loosening. "I hoped she would marry Drede," he murmured. "Are you alone?"

"Ter is with us," Sybel said. "It is fortunate for you Coren's brothers did not come. Tam, half of Eldwold must be looking for you for one purpose or another. You should not run around Eldwold as freely as though you were still herding sheep barefoot with Nyl."

"I know. But Drede would not have let me come, and I wanted to see you, to know—to know that you—that you still—"

She smiled. "That I still love you, my Tam?" she whispered. He nodded, his mouth crooking a little ruefully.

"I still have to know, Sybel." He rubbed his face wearily. "Sometimes I am still a child. Shall I take your horses?" He took the reins, murmured soothingly to the horses as he led them to the shed. Sybel dropped her face into her hands.

"I am sorry I ever brought him and Drede face to face," she said tautly.

Coren drew her hair back from her bowed face. "You could not have kept him safe forever," he said soothingly. "He was not destined by birth or the circumstances we created at Terbrec, for a quiet life."

"I would bring him back with me to Sirle except he would not want to come. He needs Drede. And I will not use Tam to punish Drede." She checked suddenly, hearing her words, and lifted her head to see the bewilderment in Coren's eyes.

"Punish Drede for what?"

She drew a breath and smiled. "Oh, I am beginning to sound like Rok or Eorth, talking about Terbrec."

"Have they been troubling you?"

"No. They have been very kind. But I do have ears, and I have heard the language of their hate." She bent to Gules Lyon, standing patiently before her, and looked deep into his golden eyes.

Is it well with you?

Well, White One, but I have heard a disturbing tale about that King. Tell me what must be done and I will do it.

Nothing. Yet. I am taking all of you to Sirle.

We expected it.

She rose, a little taut smile on her lips. Coren said softly,

"You seem so far from me sometimes. Your face changes—it is like a clear, still flame, powerful, untouchable."

"I am no farther than the sound of my name." She took his hand and they walked to the house. "Gules said they expected to be moved. I am glad Rok wants them."

"Rok, my sweet one, is shrewd." Cyrin Boar greeted the opening door and he stopped, a smile tugging at his mouth. "Cyrin. You see how I have overcome a mountain of—glass."

The silver-bristled Boar said in his sweet voice, "Have you? Or did the witch remove it herself for her own purposes?"

"No doubt I did," Sybel said quietly. "For a purpose I could not resist any longer. Cyrin, we are going to Sirle."

The Boar said privately, *Does he know to ask why?*

No. I will not have him troubled. Put a guard on your wise tongue.

Who will guard the tongue of the Wise One of Sirle when his blind eyes open?

She was silent a moment, her fingers tight on Coren's hand. *I ask only for your silence. If you cannot give it, and you wish to be free, I will free you.*

Caught between the riddle and its answer there is no freedom.

"Sybel," said Coren, and she came back to him.

"The Lord of Wisdom is at times disturbing," she said softly. "But you know that."

"Yes, I know. But not to the undisturbed mind."

She looked at him. "I am not always honest, Coren."

"I love you precisely because you are. Tell me what he said that troubled you."

"It is myself troubling myself over events that have passed. Nothing more. Like Tam, sometimes I am still a child."

Tam came in then with Ter on his shoulder. He bent to stroke Moriah at Sybel's feet. "Have you come back here to live?" he asked hopefully.

"No, Tam. I am moving my books and animals to Sirle."

His hand checked, hovering between Moriah's ears. He said softly, not looking up, "Sybel, it will be hard for me to come and see you there. But perhaps you could come sometimes to Mondor."

"Perhaps," she said gently.

"Also—" He looked up, shaking his pale hair back from his eyes. "May I please talk to you awhile?"

She glanced at Coren who said courteously, "I will sit here by the fire and talk to Cyrin."

"Thank you," Tam said and followed Sybel, his shoulders bowed, into the domed room. Gules Lyon padded behind them. Sybel sat down on the thick fur and drew Tam down beside her.

"You are growing. You are nearly as tall as I am."

He nodded, twisting the soft fur around his fingers. His pale brows drew together. "Sybel, I miss you very much, and it hurts me that—that you chose to marry Coren, not because of him, but because to other people now we are not Sybel and Tam but Sirle and Drede, who have always been enemies. Things used to be very simple, and now they are so complicated I do not know how they will end."

"I do not know either, my Tam. I only know that I will never do anything to hurt you."

His eyes rose, troubled. "Sybel, what is my father afraid of? Is it you? He will not even let me say your name."

"Tam, I have done nothing to hurt him. I have done nothing to make him afraid."

"But I have never seen him like this, and I do not know what to do to help him. I have not known him very long, and I am afraid—afraid of losing him, like I lost you."

Her brows twisted. "You have not lost me—I will love you always, no matter where you live, where I live."

He nodded a little jerkily, his mouth twitching downward. "I know. But it is different, so different now, when the people we love hate each other. I thought as long as you were here on Eld, I could come here any time, away from the noise and people in Mondor and—

just lie here by your fire with Gules, or run on the Mountain with Ter and Nyl—just for a while, and then go back home to Drede. I thought you would always be here with the animals. But now, you are going, taking them to a place where I know I cannot come. I never thought that would happen. I never thought you would marry Coren. You did not seem to like him."

"I never thought I would, either. But then I found I loved him."

"Well, I can understand that. But I do not know why Drede does not. You would never use your powers to start a war; you said so. Drede must know that, but he is so afraid of something, and sometimes I think—I think he may be lost somewhere inside himself."

She drew a breath and loosed it. "I wish you were small again, so I could hold you in my arms and comfort you. But you are grown, and you know that for some things there is no comfort."

"Oh, I know. But Sybel—sometimes I am not that grown."

She smiled and drew him against her. "Neither am I." He rested his head on her shoulder, twisted a tendril of her long hair in his fingers. "Are you happy at Mondor? Have you made friends?"

"Oh, I have cousins my age. I never knew before what cousins are. It surprised me that I have so many relatives, when here I had only you. We go hunting together—they like Ter, but they are afraid of him, and he will not let anyone hold him but me. At first they laughed at me, because I was so ignorant of many things. Maelga and you taught me to read and write but you never taught me to use a sword, or hunt with hounds, or even who was king before Drede. I have learned a great deal about Eldwold you never knew to tell me. But I learned such things on this mountain that they will never know. Are you—are you happy at Sirle?"

"Yes. I am learning things, too, about living with people that Ogam never knew to tell me."

He shifted, stirred by a restless thought, and groped for words. "Sybel. Why—why did my father say you were going to marry him? He told me one night not long ago—he said he did not mean to tell me then, because it was still a little uncertain, but he wanted to watch my face. I hugged him, I was so glad, and he laughed and then—the next evening I spoke to him about it and he—just looked at me, saying nothing. He looked ill, and—old."

"Tam—" Her voice shook slightly and she stopped. "He had no right to tell you that because I had never consented to it. Perhaps he—"

"Yes, but when did he ask you? Did he write to you?"

"No."

"I do not understand. He seemed so certain . . . Perhaps I made the mistake—I mistook something he said. I do not know. But what is he afraid of? He never laughs. He hardly talks to anyone. I thought, coming here I could find out what was troubling him, but I was wrong."

"I am sorry you are troubled about Drede, but I cannot—I cannot help you. Drede's fears are of his own making. Ask him."

"I have. He will not tell me." He reached out, put one arm around Gules, his brows knit worriedly. "I think I had better go home carefully, more carefully than I came. Drede will be angry with me, but I am glad I came. I am glad I could talk to you. I miss you, and Gules. Someday, though, I will come to Sirle."

"No."

He smiled. "I will come so quietly no one but you, Gules and Cyrin will know I am there. I will come."

"Tam, no," she said helplessly. "You do not realize—" She checked suddenly, her head turned quickly toward a drawling, bubbling wail that ascended, faded and ascended again beyond the closed door. "What—" Gules rumbled beside Tam, rose suddenly and gave a sharp, full-throated growl. Sybel rose. There was a crash beyond the door, and the murmur of men's voices.

"Coren—" she breathed. She turned, flung open the door. Gules Lyon bounded past her, came to a crouch at the fireplace, his gold tail twitching. Coren looked at Sybel over the blades of three swords held at his throat. He was unarmed, backed against the hearthstones. Moriah paced at his feet, wailing at three men who wore the black tunics with the single blood-red star of Drede's service on their breasts. Tam, beside Sybel, said quickly,

"Do not hurt him."

The guards' faces turned slowly to him, their eyes flicking between him and Moriah. One of them said between his teeth, "Prince Tamlorn, this one is of Sirle."

"Do you know them, Tamlorn?" Coren asked. A blade point bit the hollow of his throat, and he closed his mouth.

"Yes. They are my father's guards." His eyes moved back to their tense faces. "I came here to see Sybel. She did not know I was coming. I have talked to her, and I am ready to come home. Let him go."

"This is Coren of Sirle, Norrel's brother—he was at Terbrec—"

"I know, but if you hurt him I do not think you will leave this place alive."

The man glanced at Moriah, then at Gules, his golden eyes full on their faces, rumbling deep in his throat. "The King is half-mad with worry. If we let Coren loose, we will be killed by these beasts. And if Drede knows we let one of Sirle slip through our hands, we might as well be killed by them."

"Are you alone?"

"No. The others are beyond the gate. They will come if we call."

"Then no one but you will need to know that Coren and Sybel were here. I will not tell Drede."

"Prince Tamlorn, he is the King's enemy—your enemy!"

"He is Sybel's husband! And if you want to risk killing him in front of Sybel, Gules and Moriah, go ahead. I can go home by myself like I came."

Moriah screamed again, flat-eared, crouched at Coren's feet, and the blades jumped, winking. One of the guards drew his sword back suddenly. Sybel's flat voice froze the drive of it toward Moriah.

"If you do that, I will kill you."

The guard stared at her still, black eyes, sweat breaking out on his face. "Lady, we will take the Prince and go. I swear it. But how—what guarantee do we have that we will walk alive out of your house, if we let Coren go? What is the surety for our lives?"

Tam's eyes rested a moment speculatively on Coren's face. He came forward and knelt at Coren's feet beneath the swords, and put his arms around Moriah.

"I am. Now let him go."

The swords wavered, winking in the firelight, fell. Coren's breath rose soundlessly and fell.

"Thank you."

Tam looked up at him, stroking Moriah's head. "Think of it as a gift from Drede to Sirle." He rose and said to the guards, "I will come home now. But no one of you is to stay here after me, or follow Sybel and Coren when they leave. No one."

"Prince Tamlorn—we saw nothing of Sybel or Coren."

Tam sighed. "My horse is in the shed—the gray. Get him."

They left quickly, followed by the soft whisperings of Lyon, Boar and Cat. Tam went to Sybel, and she held him a moment, his face hidden in her hair.

"My Tam, you are growing as fearless and wise as Ter."

He drew away from her a little. "No. I am shaking." He smiled at her, and she kissed him quickly. He turned and hugged Gules Lyon tightly, then rose to the sound of hoofbeats at the door.

"Prince Tamlorn," Coren said soberly, "I am very grateful. And I think this gift will be a great embarrassment to the Lord of Sirle."

"I hope he is pleased," Tam said softly. "Good-bye, Sybel. I do not know when I will see you again."

"Good-bye, my Tam."

From a window, she watched him mount, Ter circling above his head, watched his straight figure swallowed by a crowd of dark-cloaked men with their fiery stars, until they had disappeared through the trees. Then she turned and went to Coren, put her arms around him, her face against his breast.

"They might have killed you before I even knew they were in my house, in spite of all my powers. Then what would Rok have said?"

He lifted her face with his hands, a smile creasing his eyes. "That I should not have to depend on my wife to save my skin."

She touched his throat. "You are bleeding."

"I know. You are shaking."

"I know."

"Sybel. Could you have killed that guard? He believed you could, and I was not sure, then, myself."

"I do not know. But if he had killed Moriah, I would have found out." She sighed. "I am glad he did not, for his sake and mine. Coren, I do not think we should stay here long. I do not trust those guards. Let us pack the books and leave."

Coren nodded. He picked up a chair that had overturned, found his sword in a corner and sheathed it.

Gules Lyon lay muttering softly by the fire. Moriah prowled back and forth in front of the door. Sybel dropped a soothing hand on the flat, black head. She looked around vaguely at the house and found a strange emptiness that seemed to lie beneath the cool white stones. She said slowly,

"It seems no longer my house . . . It seems to be waiting for another wizard, like Myk or Ogam, to begin his work here in this white silence . . ."

"Perhaps someone will come." He unfolded the big, tough grain sacks they had brought to pack the books in, and added wryly, "I hope he will have gentler memories of it than I ever will."

"I hope so, too." She gave him a tight parting hug, then went out to speak with Gyld and the Black Swan while he packed. The late afternoon turned from gold to silver, and then to ash gray. Coren finished before she returned; he went into the yard, calling her name in the wind. She came to him finally from the trees.

"I was with Gyld. I told him there would be a place for him at Sirle, and he told me he would bring his gold."

"Oh, no. I can see a glittering trail of ancient coin from here to Rok's doorstep."

"Coren, I told him we would see to it somehow . . . he will have to fly by night, when we are ready for him. I hope he does not frighten all of Rok's livestock." She glanced up at the night-scented, ashen sky, and the green-black shapes of trees. "It is getting late. What should we do? I do not think we should even stay at Maelga's house."

"No. Drede would not mind risking a war by killing me if he could trap you, take you to Mondor. If he wants that, they will return tonight to look for us."

"Then what should we do?"

"I have been thinking about that."

"The horses are tired. We cannot go far on them."

"I know."

"Well, what have you been thinking about that has put the smile in your voice?"

"Gyld."

She stared at him. "Gyld? Do you mean—ride him?"

He nodded. "Why not? You could pretend he is the Liralen. Surely he is strong enough."

"But—what would Rok say?"

"What would any man say if a dragon landed in his courtyard? Sybel, we cannot ride the horses far, and this mountain is no safe place for us tonight, wherever we are on it. You can loose the horses, call them back to Sirle when they are rested."

"But there is no place to put Gyld in Sirle."

"I will think of a place. And if I cannot, you can send him back here. Would he be willing?"

She nodded dazedly. "Oh, yes; he loves to fly. But Coren, Rok—"

"Rok would rather see us alive on Gyld than dead on Eld Mountain. If we make a slow journey back with these books, we may be followed. So let us sail home through the sky on Gyld. Sybel, there must be a silence deeper than the silence of Eld between those stars; shall we go listen to it? Come. We will throw all the stars into Sirle, then go and dance on the moon."

A smile, faint and faraway, crept onto her face. "I always wanted to fly . . ."

"So. If you cannot fly the Liralen, then make a fiery night flight on Gyld."

She called Gyld from his winter cave, and he came to her, soaring slowly above the trees, a great, dark shape against the stars. She looked deep into his green eyes.

Can you carry a man, a woman and two sacks of books on your back?

She felt a tremor of joy in his mind like a flame springing alive.

Forever.

He waited patiently while Coren secured the books on his back, wound with lengths of rope around the base of his thick neck and wings. He heaved himself up, so Coren could pass and repass the rope beneath him, and his eyes glowed like jewels in the night, and his scales winked, gold-rimmed. Coren placed Sybel between the two bags of books and sat in front of her, holding onto the rope at Gyld's neck. He turned to look at her.

"Are you comfortable?"

She nodded and caught Gyld's mind. *Do the ropes bind you anywhere?*

No.

Then go.

The great wings unfurled, black against the stars. The huge bulk lifted slowly, incredibly, away from the cold earth, through the wind-torn, whispering trees. Above the winds struck full force, billowing their cloaks, pushing against them, and they felt the immense play of muscle beneath them and the strain of wing against wind. Then came the full, smooth, joyous soar, a drowning in wind and space, a spiraling descent into darkness that flung them both beyond fear, beyond hope, beyond anything but the sudden surge of laughter that the wind tore from Coren's mouth. Then they rose again, level with the stars, the great wings pulsing, beating a path through the darkness. The full moon, ice-white, soared with them, round and wondering as the single waking eye of a starry beast of darkness. The ghost of Eld Mountain dwindled behind them; the great peak huddled, asleep and dreaming, behind its mists. The land was black beneath them, but for faint specks of light that here and there flamed in a second plane of stars. The winds dropped past Mondor, quieted, until they melted through a silence, a cool, blue-black night that was the motionless night of dreams, dimensionless, star-touched, eternal. And at last they saw in the heart of darkness beneath them the glittering torch-lit rooms of the house of the Lord of Sirle.

They came to a gentle rest in his courtyard. A horse, waiting in the yard, screamed in terror. Dogs in the hall howled. Coren dismounted stiffly, his breath catching in a laughter beyond words, and swung Sybel to the ground. She clung to him a moment, stiff with cold, and felt Gyld's mind searching for hers.

Gyld. Be still.

There are men with torches. Shall I—

No. They are friends. They just did not expect us tonight. No one will try to harm us. Gyld, that was a flight beyond hope.

It pleased you.

I am well pleased.

"Rok!" Coren called to his brother's torchlit figure moving toward them down the steps. The dogs swarmed growling between his legs. The children jammed the doors behind him, then scattered in a wave before Ceneth and Eorth. "We have a guest!"

"Coren," Rok said, transfixed by the lucent, inscrutable eyes. "What in the name of the Above and the Below are we going to do with it?"

Coren caught one of the dogs before it nipped at Gyld's wing. "I have thought of that, too," he said cheerfully. "We can store it in the wine cellar."

NINE

They sat late with Rok, Ceneth and Eorth, until the great hall quieted and the dogs had gone to sleep at their feet. Coren told of their meeting with Tam and Drede's guards, and Rok listened silently, whirling a wine cup slowly between forefinger and thumb. He grunted when Coren finished.

"The boy is soft, yet. I wonder what Drede himself would have done."

"He would have done what I wanted him to," Sybel said. Rok's tawny eyes flicked to her face.

"Could you have controlled all of them?"

"No. They could have overwhelmed us, but it would not have been a pleasant encounter for them."

"But you could control the King."

"Rok," Coren murmured, and Rok's eyes dropped. He leaned back in his chair.

"Well. I am thankful you are safe. It was foolish of me to think of you for a moment as simply a man and his wife who could move safely as children through Eldwold, and to let you go alone."

Coren shrugged. "It was best that you did. There would have been a small war in Sybel's house if Eorth and Herne had been with us, and we would all be licking our wounds in Mondor by now, including the animals. Besides, even if Eorth had kept his temper, he probably would have broken his neck falling off Gyld on the way home."

Eorth refilled his cup. "At least, I would have had enough sense not to let myself get trapped in a corner by three of Drede's men. They must have made enough noise riding up the hill to warn you."

Coren flushed. "I know," he said. "I should have heard them. I was distracted. Cyrin was telling me about the time he met the witch Carodin in her doorless tower and answered six out of her seven riddles and discovered even she could not answer the seventh."

Eorth looked at him bewilderedly. "A Boar told you all that?"

"He talks."

"Oh, Coren, you have told us ridiculous things, but—"

"It is not ridiculous. It is true. Eorth, you never could see farther than the sword in your hand—"

"Well, that is as far as any man needs to see in this land." He appealed to Sybel. "Is he lying?"

"He never lies."

He looked at her incredulously. Rok said, with a grunt of laughter, "Eorth, do not start a fight on my hearth. I never would have believed Coren would ride a Dragon to my doorstep, but he did and I do, now. And I am also beginning to think twice about other things he has said."

Coren reached across the table for Sybel's hand. "You see what a poor reputation I had before you married me."

"So. You married me for my animals. I always knew it."

"I married you because you never laughed at me. Except when I asked you to marry me."

Eorth leaned back in his chair and grinned. "She laughed? Tell us about that, Coren."

"No."

"I laughed because I thought you had sent him to marry me," Sybel said. "Then, when I realized he loved me, I stopped laughing."

Ceneth rose, moved to the fire. The great house was still about them; shadows fell like tapestry from the walls.

"If you are not careful, Eorth, Sybel will have Gyld leave you naked on top of Eld Mountain and no one will miss you."

"I am sorry."

"You are not. You are jealous that you did not marry a woman with a dragon."

"Now we have one in our wine cellar," Rok murmured. "I wonder what our father would have said about that."

Eorth gave a snort of laughter. "He would have quit drinking. I thought of something a moment ago."

"Did you?" Ceneth said wonderingly. "What?"

"That if Sybel had a daughter, she could marry Tamlorn, control him, and in two generations the Sirle Lords could be Eldwold Kings."

"I hardly think Tam would wait fifteen years to get married," Rok said dryly.

"He could marry into Sirle anyway," Ceneth said. "Herne's daughter Vivet is twelve in summer."

"Drede would never permit it."

"So? The boy could melt Drede like wax."

"And who in Sirle is to melt Tam to this plan?"

"Sybel, of course."

Coren's hand came down sharply on the table. The wine quivered in their cups. He looked at the three silent men: Rok, big, gold-maned; Ceneth with his sleek black hair and cat-calm eyes; Eorth, slow, and leaf-bright and powerful. He lifted his hand from the table and closed it. Eorth said, flushed,

"I am sorry. I was babbling."

"Yes."

"We all were." Ceneth troubled the fire a moment with his foot. Then he turned, dropped a hand on Coren's shoulder. "It will not happen again."

Coren sighed, his face loosening. "Yes, it will. I know this house. And I know what talk is worth these days. Like a dragon flight, it comes to nothing in the end but sleep."

"Harsh, but true," Rok said. They were silent awhile. The fire dwindled to a single flame that danced above the embers. Eorth yawned, his teeth winking white as Moriah's.

"It is late," he said surprisedly. Ceneth nodded.

"I am going to bed." He stopped beside Sybel, took her hand and kissed it. "Lady, be patient with us."

She smiled up at him. "You make it easy to be patient."

He left them. They sat finishing their wine, while the shadows lengthened and locked over their heads. Coren put his empty cup down, swallowing a yawn.

"Coren, go to bed," Sybel said. "You look tired."

"Come with me."

"In a moment. I want to talk to Rok about Gyld."

"Always Rok. I will wait."

"And then I want a bath."

"Oh." He pushed his chair back and leaned across the table to kiss the top of her head. "Do not keep Rok up too long. He is an old man and needs his sleep."

"Old— At least I am not getting so slow and deaf I am easy game to any fool in Drede's service."

"Three fools," Coren said. "It took three. Good night."

"Good night," Rok said. Beside him, Eorth's head drooped, his cup dangling empty from his hands. Rok took it from him and set it on the table. "Eorth." He began to snore softly. Rok turned away from him, his mouth crooked.

"I am sorry if we troubled you tonight. Coren is right, though: since Drede stopped us at Terbrec, we talk a good deal and do little." He paused a moment. "What is it you wanted to tell me?"

Sybel's eyes lifted to his face. The hall was dim around them but for the flame of a last torch; Eorth's snoring sounded weak against the great rising of silent, ancient stone. She leaned toward Rok, her eyes dark, unwavering on his face as the black, moonlit pools of Fyrbolg.

"Something," she said finally, "that I have never told any man."

Rok was silent. Eorth was silent, too, a moment; he caught a sudden breath midsnore and woke himself up, blinking at them.

"Eorth, go to bed," Rok said impatiently, and Eorth heaved himself to his feet.

"All right."

Rok watched him go. Then he turned back to Sybel, his eyes narrowed.

"Tell me."

Sybel folded her hands on the table. "Did Coren tell you about the wizard who called me?"

Rok nodded. "He said you had been captured—called—by a very powerful wizard who was attracted to you, and that the wizard died and you came back free. He did not tell me how the wizard died."

"Let that be for a moment. What Coren does not know is that the wizard was paid by Drede to take me, and to make me—obedient to Drede, so that Drede could marry me without fearing me."

"How—obedient?"

Her mouth twitched a little, steadied. "He was paid to destroy a part of my mind, the part that chooses and wills of its own. I would have retained most of my powers, but they would have been subject to Drede. I was to be made—content with Drede."

Rok's lips parted. "Could he have done that?"

"Yes. He held—he held my mind so completely, more completely than any man holds his own mind. I would have been controlled by Drede; I would have done whatever he wanted without question or hope of question, and I would have been happy, afterward, that I had pleased Drede. That, Drede wanted." Her taut hands loosened; one lifted, cut the air. "For that, I will destroy him."

Rok sat back in his chair, the breath easing from him soundlessly. "Is that why you married Coren?" he asked suddenly. "As part of your revenge?"

"Yes."

"You do not love him?" he asked almost wistfully.

"I love him." Her hands eased apart then. "I love him," she repeated softly. "He is kind and good and wise, all those things I am not, and if I lost him, I would hunger for those things in him. For that reason, I do not want him to know what is—what is in my heart. He might hate me for this. I do not—I do not like myself so much these days. But I want Drede to suffer. I want him to know what dread and hopelessness I knew. He is learning a little of it now. Tam said he is beginning to be afraid, and with good reason. I want war between Sirle and Drede, and I want Drede powerless. I will help you under two conditions."

"Name them," Rok breathed.

"That Coren will not know I am involved. And that Tam is not used in any way against Drede. For that, I will call the Lords of Niccon and Hilt to side with you against Drede; I will use my own animals against Drede, and I will give you a king's treasure for the gathering and arming of men."

Rok gazed at her wordlessly. She saw the muscles of

his throat move as he swallowed. "You yourself are a dream come true, Lady," he whispered. "Where will you get the treasure?"

"From Gyld. He has amassed enough gold through the centuries to arm every man and child in Eldwold. If I ask him, he will give me part of it. You see, Ter was captured, too, that day, and he watched powerless himself, while Drede and Mithran spoke of their plan. When I came to Eld Mountain today, every animal there knew what had been done to us."

"But how did you escape that wizard, if he was so powerful?"

"Rommalb killed him."

"Rommalb—" She saw the memories flick in his eyes. "The nightwalker— How?"

"He—crushed him."

Rok's face was shocked, motionless in the firelight. "That is what Coren met on your hearth?"

She nodded. "It was not a pleasant meeting, but Coren did what—what few men have ever done."

"What?"

"He survived." She stirred, her hands stretching taut on the table. "I never meant for that to happen; it was Cyrin's doing, and I was terrified. But Coren is wiser than I dreamed he could be."

"So he must be—wiser than we all dreamed. Why do you not set this Rommalb at Drede?"

"Because I want a slow revenge. I want him to know what is being done to him and why, and who is responsible. The things he fears most in the world are the power and energy of Sirle, and me. He came to Mithran's tower that day expecting to find a woman who would smile and take his hand and do his bidding. Instead he found that woman gone and a great wizard lying broken on the floor. Since that day he has been afraid. Now, with your help, I will overwhelm him with his fears."

His head moved slowly from side to side. "You are merciless."

"Yes. If you choose to refuse me, I will go to bed and we will never speak of this again. But with or without Sirle, it will be done."

"You have such things involved with this—Coren's love, Tamlorn's. Do you want to risk them?"

"I have thought deep in the night, night after night, about this plan. I know the risks. I know that if Coren finds out how I have used him, or if Tam suspects that I am destroying his father, they will be hurt past bearing, and I will lose all that I value in this world. But I told you tonight what I have decided."

"Are you sure?"

She held his eyes. "It will be done."

He drew a soft breath and loosed it. "I think it will be done with Sirle."

The building of the gardens for the animals began with the softening of the earth in spring and progressed into the long summer. One by one Sybel called the animals to Sirle: first the Black Swan to take its place in a small, glass-clear lake filled with smooth stones and fire-bright fish. She went to meet it as it descended slowly over the garden, and came to glide without a ripple, night-black and regal, over the still waters. Its voice ran smooth, melodious through her thoughts.

It is small, but pleasing.

Rok, said Sybel, *is going to have a white fountain put in the middle.*

The shape, Sybel?

Two swans in flight, soaring upward, with their beaks touching.

Yes. And that matter concerning you?

It will be settled. Soon.

I am in readiness, when you have need of me.

She called Gyld from his corner in the dark, damp

wine cellar and he fell asleep again in a grotto shaded by trees, cooled by a vein of the Slinoon trained beneath the wall that danced past his cave into the Swan's lake. Jewels, cups and gold pieces past value winked dully in the shadows around him, for he had given Sybel the path to his mountain cave, and Rok had sent Eorth, Bor and Herne secretly to bring his gold. They had returned, three days after he sent them, exhausted, overladen and awestricken.

"We could not bring it all," Bor said to Rok and Sybel. He rubbed his weary eyes as though at a vision for which there were no words. "Rok, we waded ankle-deep in places through silver pieces. There were the bones of three dead men, and one wore a king's crown. And that is the beast we put so blithely into our wine cellar."

"You have nothing to fear from him," Sybel said. "He is old, and he wants nothing now but his dreams, and his gold securely about him. He is pleased with his cave."

"You could buy a kingdom with that gold," Herne said, his blue eyes gleaming in his arched, restless face. A corner of Rok's mouth lifted faintly.

"Yes."

She called the Lyon and the great, green-eyed Cat next, and they came by night, gleaming, velvet beneath the moonlight across the Sirle fields. Sybel met them at the gate, opened it for them, and they passed through softly into the garden, the grass whispering beneath them, the blossoming trees white and still against the night sky.

By winter there will be a warm place built for you, she said. *I will miss you wandering in and out of my rooms. Perhaps by winter they will learn not to fear you. This place is small, but it is private and no one should disturb you.*

Gules Lyon lay down in the long grass at her feet.

Moriah prowled soft as a shadow through the night, while the Black Swan drifted drowsing through moonshot waters.

The Lord of Sirle has done much for you, White One, said Gules. *Have you spoken to him yet?*

Yes. I offered him Eldwold. He accepted.

Gules gave a rumble, deep in his throat. *Good.*

Coren came to see them the next morning. He brought his brothers; they stood together silently, watching Gules tear open the haunch of a deer Coren had shot for him. Ceneth sucked breath between his teeth.

"You control that?"

Sybel nodded. "In the mountains, most of the time they do their own hunting, since the gardens were wide. But here, there are so many things—farmers, horses, cattle—that would be frightened by their comings and goings."

"I will assign men to hunt for them," Rok said, and her face cleared.

"Thank you. Now I will give them your names."

She called the two Cats to her, and the Black Swan; and the men were still beneath the still gazes of the three, while Sybel moved among them, one by one, naming each.

Rok. Bor. Eorth. Herne. Ceneth. Remember them. Guard them.

"Where is Cyrin?" Coren said. "Have you called him?"

"No."

He looked at her, surprised. "Surely the place is ready for him. Call him now, Sybel. He must be lonely by himself. He will think you do not want him."

She drew a breath. "I hope he will be happy here." She lifted her face toward the wind and sent the final call across the land, and felt Cyrin, beneath a tree, rise in answer.

"Cyrin," Eorth said to Herne. "The Boar. Coren says he talks."

"I believe it," Herne said simply. "After what we have seen these past days, I am willing to believe anything."

Sybel spoke with Rok again that night, in private when the household lay asleep around them and the dogs stretched dreaming at their feet. The scent of early summer rose from the crushed blossoms and new rushes on the stone floor, from the fields lying night-damp, with seedlings breaking the earth.

"I have told Ceneth and Bor that you will help us against Drede," Rok said. "Eorth and Herne know only that we plot a war: they will not question how or why, but Ceneth and Bor have wits and use them. They know Sirle might overthrow the King alone, but not the combined forces of the King and the Lords of Niccon and Hilt. So they asked me, of course, where we would get the strength. I explained. They approved." He paused a moment, sipping wine. "We were reared to battle, Sybel. Our grandfather laid the seventy-day siege of Mondor, and our father, not much older than Tamlorn, then, fought beside him. Since Norrel's death at Terbrec we have wanted revenge, but Niccon sided with Drede at that battle, and Horst of Hilt threw up his hands in despair and waited for the outcome of the war over his dead daughter. So we have not been sure of support."

"Would Horst of Hilt fight, do you think, for the wrong Drede has done Laran's daughter; or would he fight for Rianna's child, Drede's son?"

Rok shook his head. "I would not like to make a choice like that myself. Coren is right, I suspect: he will fight for the man he thinks will win. In this case: Drede."

"So. I will persuade him otherwise." She lifted her

eyes to Rok's face. "And the Lord of Niccon. When shall I bring them to you?"

"Let me begin gathering men. Drede will turn to Hilt and Niccon, ask for support, and they will no doubt give it to him. Then, Sybel, you may call them, and Drede will watch his support drain like water through his fingers . . . I think he will know then who is behind the Sirle war."

She nodded. "And Coren. Does he know what you are planning?"

"He will, when Herne and Eorth begin to babble. No doubt he will think I am mad, until he sees Derth of Niccon ride into our courtyard."

"He must not know where the money comes from."

"No."

She stirred a little. "I am afraid."

"Of Coren?"

"Yes. I am afraid of the look in his eyes the day he finds out what game I am playing with Sirle."

"It is our game as much as yours. You gave us a choice, and we took it. Besides, do you think if you told him what Drede had done to you he would not want revenge of his own? Why will you not tell him?"

"No."

"But why? He is your husband—he would surely support your revenge. He has no love for Drede."

Her mouth tightened. "I will not draw Coren into the whirlpool of my anger and hatred. No revenge of his making could satisfy me, and it is purposeless involving him in mine. I want—I want to keep him free of hate. He—the night we flew the Dragon, we dropped downward suddenly, rushing toward darkness as though toward the endless deep of the night, blind, helpless, as you are when there is nothing left of you but the unhidden center of yourself—and from the core of him came a living, joyous laughter. Lost in his own hate for Drede, he could not have laughed like that. He may fight in this war simply because if he refused to fight for my sake and you died at battle, he would never forgive himself for not being with you. But I will give him no great cause to fight for. I will not drag him through his grief and bitterness again. He has given me so much love. At least I can give him that one protection."

Rok looked at her silently a moment, his lips parted. "I doubt if it is possible," he said at last, gently. "But I love you for trying."

She went the next afternoon to the room high in the house that Rok had given her and sat for a while in the silence, stilling her thoughts, searching in far and secret places for the elusive Liralen. Her books stood on shelves against the walls, the metal and jewels on their backs searched by fingers of light that came from windows facing three directions. Lost to Sirle, sending thread after thread of a call that drifted always idly, unattached, unanswered, she did not see Coren until he knelt before her where she sat on cushions, and spoke her name.

"Sybel."

She drew her mind back from regions farther than she had ever gone, and looked at him silently, blinking a moment.

"Coren. I am sorry—I did not hear you come in. I was calling the Liralen. I am looking in places so far they have no names, and yet I think it must be closer; I think sometimes it must have answered, but I did not hear it."

"Sybel—" He paused, his brows drawn in a rare frown. She reached out, traced the lines of it on his face.

"What is it?"

He took her hand, folded her fingers in his. "Sybel, my brothers are babbling of war. Rok has sent messengers to our border farmers to mend their armor and shoe their war-horses, and he is sending Bor and Eorth to the lesser lords of Eldwold who are pledged through lands and favors to Sirle. I have asked Rok why, and why again, and he laughs and says that Drede is afraid of us or they would have killed me that day on Eld Mountain. I have asked him what hope of support he has, why he would risk our lives and lands for a battle that will be only another Terbrec, and he says that he will dangle the bait of power in front of Lord Horst, who is kin to both you and Tamlorn. He told me he did not expect me to fight against Drede, the father of the boy my wife reared and loved, but I cannot—I cannot sit quietly while they go to their deaths. So—I have come to you, to see what look is in your eyes when I tell you I will fight."

She drew a deep breath, her eyes wide on his face. "It is sudden, this war."

"Too sudden. Rok says Drede will be weakened by the unexpectedness of it, but I think that bitter man is prepared to fight every day of his life, and that the Lion of Sirle is moving in a dreamworld. Sybel, are you angry with me? You know I want no war against Drede and Tam, especially not such a futile, hopeless thing as this. But if I stay here safe within these walls, and if my brothers die in battle, I will see their faces, hear their voices calling to me in my dreams until I die. Can you forgve me? Or can you give me a reason, one I can cling to even through my brothers' deaths, not to fight?"

"No," she whispered. "Only that all my joy will be gone from the earth if you are killed in this war. Coren, perhaps the Lion is not dreaming. Perhaps Rok is right and Sirle will defeat Drede, and no one will be killed."

He shook his head, his face pained, hopeless. "Sybel, men will die; perhaps not my brothers, but men of Sirle. At Terbrec, I heard their broken, weary voices weeping of their wounds while I fought, until I did not know anymore, in the dust, heat and blinding leap of metal, if they were truly men's voices, or the broken, crying voices of my own thoughts that could never again be coherent. It will be the same thing all over again, now. Rok is mad. I told him so, but he simply told me I did not have to fight. But he knows I will."

"He does not seem mad," she said gently. "Perhaps he knows something you do not know."

"I hope so, for all our sakes." He lifted a hand, traced the line of her hair. "You are not angry. I thought you would be. I thought you might leave me, go back to Eld."

"And what would there be for me at Eld but an empty house? Coren, I knew when I married you that one day, sooner or later, I would have to watch you leave me, I would have to wait here quietly within these stones like Rok's wife and Eorth's wife, and not know if I would ever see you again. I just did not expect it now, so soon."

"I did not dream Rok would ever do this; I thought we would live peacefully for years before anything such as this would happen."

"I know. But things—things have simply woven together into a pattern, and now I cannot tell anymore where the thread of events began. So you must do what you must, and I—what I must."

"I am sorry," he whispered helplessly.

"No. The only thing you will have to be sorry for is if you die, and then beware because I will follow you."

"No."

"Yes. I will not let you wander among the stars alone."

He smiled a little, swallowing. He touched her lips, then kissed them gently. Then he held her tightly, crushed against him, gathering her hair in his hands, and she listened to the slow life beat of his heart. They sat silent, motionless in the fall of sunlight, until

Coren's hold loosened. He stood up, helped her up. Then he said, looking over her shoulder out the window,

"Sybel, Cyrin is coming across the fields. We should go down and open the gate for him."

The silver Boar met them at the postern, his tusks shining in the hot noon. He stood a moment, panting at Sybel's feet, looking at her out of his red eyes, and then he spoke to her in his flute-smooth voice,

"The giant Grof was hit in one eye by a stone, and that eye turned inward so that it looked into his mind and he died of what he saw there."

Sybel stiffened. Coren stared incredulously at the great Boar. His head turned, flashing, toward Sybel, and she saw the startled question in his eyes. She found answer for neither of them, so she simply held open the gate, and Cyrin passed through into her garden.

TEN

She moved the Lords of Niccon and Hilt like chess pieces across Eldwold, from their heartlands to the house of the Lord of Sirle, until they stood blinking as at a dream while the smiling Rok welcomed them into his house. Rok's hall began to fill at noon and evenings with men who sat at their meals in shirts of leather and steel, with knives at their belts, and who spoke with their mouths full of battles they had seen and the scars they had taken as remembrances. The outer yards rang with the constant hollow beat of hammer as swords were forged, shields repaired, spear points welded to lengths of pale, straight ash, carts built, harness and gear of the great-hooved war-horses mended. All this the Lord Horst of Hilt, and in his turn, Lord Derth of Niccon, a fiery-haired young man who had sworn life and family to Drede's service, saw and looked within themselves to find good. Derth of Niccon, arriving a week after the Lord of Hilt, said rather plaintively at Rok's hearth, with a cup of wine in his hand,

"I did not realize you had so many followers, or I would not have pledged everything to Drede. But I did that because of Terbrec."

"I do not intend a second Terbrec," Rok said, his

eyes calm, gleaming faintly below the gold mane of hair. A little away from them, an ivory-haired woman sat quietly, needlework in her hands, her black eyes never moving from Derth's face, and to him she was little more than a shadow that did not impress itself into his memory. Derth sighed, tapping his cup with a fingernail.

"I can give you five hundred mounted men and three or four times as many on foot."

"The Lord of Hilt offered me less."

"His lands are divided—part of them Carn of Hilt captured during the seventy-day siege of Mondor, and the men on them are claiming their old allegiance to the King."

"So? No doubt we can deal with them. Horst is too old for these games. I pity him."

Derth snorted into his cup. "Pity Drede, if you must. I have heard Horst was pledged to Drede, too, first, before he turned to you."

Rok's brows rose in polite surprise; he refrained from comment.

Coren, weaving his way through the benches of men at their noon meal, caught sight of the red-haired lord and stood still midstep. Ceneth, with a faint smile, turned from his food and pushed a full cup into Coren's hand. Coren stared down at him.

"Do you see who that is?"

"Yes."

"Derth of Niccon. Ceneth, how did Rok get him here? Drede gave his father lands and gold for the work he did at Terbrec. What is Derth doing sitting at our hearth?"

Ceneth shrugged. "Doubtless he heard the Lord of Hilt had turned to Sirle's side and discovered he would rather fight with Hilt than against it."

"But, Ceneth—" He groped for words, found them

inaccessible for once, and drank instead. Then he saw Sybel and went to her.

"I have been looking for you everywhere."

She blinked up at him, startled, the thread of her call broken. "Coren—" Beside Rok, the Lord of Niccon rubbed his eyes with his fingers.

"I feel very confused," he commented. Rok refilled his cup.

"You are tired from your ride." He turned, tugged Coren away from Sybel. "Eorth was looking for you; it seemed important."

"I want to take Sybel riding. She is not used to all this babble and din." He paused a moment, then asked slowly, "What are you doing here with Rok and Lord Derth?"

"Oh, she said vaguely, her thoughts rushing like birds ahead of her. "I wanted to talk to Rok."

Rok added smoothly, "She was worried. Eorth is talking about riding Gyld into battle."

"What!"

"She could not talk him out of it. Perhaps you can."

The Lord of Niccon leaned across Rok to stare at Sybel. "Are you Sybel? I have heard about you . . ."

She smiled at him sweetly, holding his eyes, and he sank back in his chair. Coren said grimly,

"Perhaps if I tie him to his horse he will understand. Sybel, wait for me—"

He turned and made his way back into the crowd. Rok sighed softly and turned to the subdued Lord of Niccon.

"Now. The siege of my grandfather failed because he did not have the men to deal with supplies coming down the Slinoon River into Mondor. This time, I want men of Sirle and Niccon attacking by water, sailing through to the heart of the city and attacking within. We will need boats. Niccon is in the lake country of Eldwold. Can you build boats for three hundred men, and gather men to sail them?"

The Lord of Niccon stared at him like a man asleep with his eyes open and nodded. "Yes."

"I will bear the cost for them."

"When do you want them?"

Rok smiled a little. "Soon, but there is no great hurry. I am sure Drede will wait for us."

He put the Lord of Niccon into Lynette's care when he had done with him, and she took him, puzzled, half-drunk, but enthused, to the same chamber where the Lord of Hilt had slept a week before. Sybel rose and paced a little through the empty hall; Rok watched her.

"What are you thinking?"

"If I bring the animals into the battlefield, will Coren see them?"

"He can hardly avoid seeing Gyld. But the others . . . In the crush of men, the close flash and thrust of battle, he will probably notice nothing he does not expect to see. Why would you risk them, though? There is no need."

A little, tight smile played about her mouth. She said softly, "The Prince Ilf went one day with fifty men to capture the lovely daughter of Mak, Lord of Macon; on the way Ilf saw a black mountain Cat with fur that gleamed like a polished jewel. The Cat looked at him out of her green eyes, and Ilf gave chase and no one saw him or his fifty men on earth again. The three strong sons of King Pwill went with their friends hunting one day, and saw a silver-bristled Boar with great tusks white as the breasts of their highborn wives, and Pwill waited for them to come home, waited seven days and seven nights, and of those fifteen young men only his youngest son ever returned from that hunt. And he returned half-mad."

Rok stared at her. "So will Drede be, seeing parts of his army vanish before his eyes. Will they do this for you?"

"Yes."

"Even the Boar? You said he did not approve."

She traced a meaningless design on an oaken tables with her forefinger. "He will do this if I command him to. The Swan I will send to Tam, to fly with him to Eld Mountain if at any moment his life is in danger. And Ter Falcon will guard Tam."

"And Gyld?"

Her eyes narrowed in a slow smile. "Gyld will bring Drede to me."

Rok's head moved once from side to side. "Now," he said softly, "I am beginning to pity Drede."

There was a step without. They turned to see Coren, his hair bright in the summer light, pause at the open doors, one hand on the stones. He looked at Rok and asked softly,

"Why did you lie to me about Eorth?"

Rok sighed. "Because I was telling lies to the Lord of Niccon, and I did not want you embarrassing me with the truth."

"You are lying to me now." He stepped forward into the quiet, sun-streaked hall, came to stand so close to Rok there was scarcely a hand's breadth between them. "Why did you need my wife beside you while you told lies to Derth of Niccon, who could barely recognize truth if it leaped like a salmon from the bottom of his wine cup?"

"Coren," Sybel said, but his eyes did not move from Rok's face.

"There are things I do not understand about this war you plot. There are things I am not sure, now, that I want to understand. How you persuaded that old man, Horst of Hilt to your side, when last winter you sent me to him and I found him terrified of Drede, wanting only to live out his days in peace, to forget his unfortunate daughter and the chaos she made of Drede's love. Why Derth of Niccon, whose older brother you killed at Terbrec, would come and sit beside you, drink your wine and plan a war with you? Why you planned this war before you even spoke to them? And why, if there are simple reasons for all these things, you did not have the courtesy or the regard for me to tell me before I had to ask?"

Rok was silent. He drew a long breath, his eyes hidden in his still face, and Coren's hands closed at his sides.

"Do not lie to me again," he whispered.

"Coren," Sybel said. His eyes moved slowly from Rok's face to hers, and she saw in them the dark, reluctant blooming of his doubt. For a long moment they stood motionless, their eyes locked, still as the sunlight falling against the crushed summer flowers on the hall floor. Then Coren moved away from Rok, went out of the hall, down the steps to the yard. Rok watched his head gleam in and out of the shadows. Then he heard the sharp catch of Sybel's breath and turned.

"What did you do?" he breathed incredulously.

"I did not mean to—" Her hands rose, covering her mouth. "I did not mean to— Not to Coren—not Coren. It was—I did not know what to say to him—and it was so easy—"

"But what did you do?"

"I made him forget what he saw today, what he asked you. I am sorry." She began to tremble suddenly, and tears slid glittering between her fingers. "I am so sorry. It was so—easy."

"Sybel—"

"I am frightened."

"Sybel." He went to her, held her gently by the shoulders. "It was no worse than lying to him."

"It was! It was! I took things from his mind—as—Mithran would have taken them from mine—it was a thing no one should do, in either love or hate—"

"Sh. Sybel, you are tired from the work this morning, and you forgot what you were doing. There is no great harm done. It is better for him this way, and you will never do it again."

"I am afraid."

"Hush, you did little harm, little more than lying—you will not do it again."

"No."

"Then do not worry."

Her eyes, staring wide out of the empty doorway, came back to his face. "You do not understand. He—he thinks I am honest. And I have lied to him since the day I married him." She looked down suddenly at his hands, as though realizing for the first time that he was holding her. She pulled away from him, ran to the door.

She saw Coren walking out the main gate toward the open fields and ran after him through the yard, past the billowing smoke of the smithy, the pound of hammers from the carpenter's shop, the startled faces of farmers and warriors, moving aside so she could pass. Coren heard her call finally and stopped on the dusty road. He waited for her, the smile on his face fading as she neared him. He lifted his hands, caught her, and she crept close to him, her head against his shoulder.

"Hold me, Coren," she whispered, and his arms formed a circle of peace about her. He felt her trembling.

"What is it?"

"Nothing. Just hold me."

"You have been crying."

"I know."

"What has made you cry?"

Her eyes opened, dark, to the hot fields and the shimmering sky. She felt his hold tighten. "I was thinking," she whispered, and the words burned through her throat, "of myself without you . . . and how I could not bear it."

"Sybel, what can I say to comfort you? There will be no comfort in this war until it is over. But you were right somehow: Rok is not mad and there is, through some magic I do not understand, a chance for Sirle. So perhaps it will be brief—though that cannot comfort you much either, where Tam is concerned. But I am so glad that you still care enough to cry about me in spite of this."

"I care. I care." She stirred finally and his arms dropped. He glanced around puzzledly at the green fields.

"I forgot why I came out here. You frightened me, running toward me with your hair like a silver wake and tears on your face."

"Yes. I made you forget," she whispered. "I am sorry."

He put his arm around her, and they walked back together to the house, black crows fluttering upward from the fields around them as they passed.

She spoke to her animals that evening. She had called Ter Falcon from Mondor; he came in the twilight, shooting like a star from the blue-black sky. He perched among the rich green leaves of the summer trees, and she said to him,

Ter. Tell me of Drede.

He is a man afraid to the core and the bone, said the glittering-eyed Falcon. *He shouts in his sleep at night, and a torch burns always in his room. He is afraid of the night shadows. A fear beyond the fear of battle grows behind his eyes like thick, winter ice. There are whispers that he is going mad, but he contains himself, saying little.*

And Tam?

Tam watches. He takes me with him everywhere; he talks to me late at night and falls asleep sometimes still

talking. He wants you to help Drede. He told me to ask you. He is desperate.

And you?

I am ready.

Listen then for any words that may help Rok. When the moment comes, I want you at Tam's side, protecting him. She lifted her head, called the Swan to her. Gules came to lie at her feet, and Moriah beside him, and she woke Gyld in his cave with a touch of her mind. Cyrin Boar came to her between the trees, glowing in the darkness. For a long moment that tested the strength and sinew of her mind, straining concentration to its limits, she held the six proud, restless minds at once.

Listen to me. When the Lord of Sirle and his brothers ride out of Sirle to battle, Ter and the Swan of Tirlith will fly then to Mondor, to Tam. The Swan will be ready at any moment to fly him to Eld Mountain, if there is danger to him. Ter, I want you to keep Tam safe. Moriah, Gules and Cyrin, you will appear to Drede's army, before the battle, during the battle, luring men away with the magic of your eyes, the beauty of you. Gyld, I will keep with me until Drede is finished, and then Gyld will bring the King to me at the wizard's tower in Mondor.

At all times keep yourselves discreetly out of sight until you see fit to move. Stay away from Rok's men. Put yourself into no unnecessary danger, except for Tam's sake and—if you choose—for Coren's sake. Ter, stay away from Drede. Unless he is killed in battle, I want him brought to me alive.

The wind sighed briefly in the quiet night. She paused a moment, weary, then trained her mind once more into theirs.

The legends told of you are countless, but all of them old. What you do in this battle, harpists will sing of for years, touching their silver strings with wonder, and your proud, ancient names will echo again within the stone walls of men's courts, fine-sounding as new-polished gold, honored and revered.

She paused again, feeling in one moment the swift, pulsing beat of Ter's thoughts, the jewels of the hidden memories in Gules' mind, Moriah's mind, the serene acquiescence of the Black Swan's moonlit mind, the twists of Gyld's fiery brain, the constant play of riddle upon riddle in Cyrin's mind, woven out of the unending threads of his thoughts. She loosed them, spent, and as they waited quietly around her, she rested a moment. Then she took their questions.

Do you want Drede's men destroyed? Moriah asked. *Or returned after a suitable time?*

I do not want their lives. Run them in circles a while, then let them go.

Why will you not let me fight? Gyld asked. *I could scatter Drede's army with a single flight through it.*

No. You would frighten Rok's men, too. Wait patiently with me.

There may be men guarding Eld Mountain, the Swan said. *Where then, Sybel?*

Then bring him to Sirle. But take him first to the mountain and wait for me, if there is no danger.

What will you do with Drede? Ter asked.

Nothing. I want only to look into his eyes when I am done with him, when he has nothing—neither power, nor rank, nor even Tam to comfort him. Mithran was fortunate compared to him. By then, he may be mad.

And what will you do with yourself afterward? Cyrin asked.

Sybel, looking into his red eyes, was silent. The leaves rustled in the wind above her as at a sudden breath, then stilled. She whispered at last to herself, "I do not know."

There came a few days later to Rok's hall a slender, long-nosed woman with rich rings on her fingers and her white hair in a thousand untidy curls. She passed into it so quietly that she reached Rok's elbow unnoticed as he sat at his meal, with Lynette on one side of him and Bor at the other, and she tugged at his sleeve. He turned, startled, to meet the iron-gray eyes.

"Where is Sybel?"

"Sybel?" He sent a glance down the table. "She left, I think, with Coren. Perhaps they are— Old woman, who are you? Will you sit with us? I did not hear you come in."

Her wandering eyes came back to him. "Oh, I am the sharp-eyed old crow of Eld Mountain. And you—you I think are the Lion of Sirle. Such a lovely family you have, such peach-colored children and lordly brothers. I have had such a walk from Eld Mountain."

"You walked!" Rok exclaimed. Beside him, Bor rose courteously.

"Sit down, Lady. Eat with us."

She smiled at him, her hands fluttering to touch her hair. "So kind . . ." she murmured and sat. "Oh, my feet. I am Maelga, Sybel's mother." At her right hand, Ceneth coughed over his wine and she turned to him. "I am the only mother she ever had. You may not think a mountain witch would make a very good mother."

"I am sure you were better than nothing," Ceneth said weakly. Rok caught his eye, and he reddened.

"I am not so sure of that," Maelga said candidly, searching through a plate of sugared fruits and nuts. "Otherwise, I would not have had to walk all the way from Eld Mountain to Sirle to find out why Cyrin Boar came snorting to me with such a tale I could not believe . . ." She caught Rok's swift glance from side to side over the rows of preoccupied faces. "Oh, is it a secret?"

"Old woman, what do you want?" Rok said softly and she sighed.

"Dried, sweetened apricots . . . I am a child with sweet things. You see, Rok, I have done—oh, things by twilight, dim things by candlelight that are spoken of best by hushed voices. I am an old woman with a weakness for meddling, and people give me rings and soft furs and bright ribbons. I weave on a small loom with threads of simple colors. But Sybel—now there is a weave, her weave, with a loom the size of Eldwold and threads of living scarlet."

"It is her choice."

"Yes, but it frightens me in my old heart. It frightens Cyrin, too, and he such a wise old Boar. Rok, when you look at her you see a beautiful, strong-willed woman whose power is the star of fortune over Sirle. And I see a child with a festering hurt that eventually will be the death of her."

Rok set his cup softly on the table. Maelga looked at him, her white brows arched over her sharp eyes, her chin resting on her ringed fingers. He was silent a moment, his fingers tapping the silver.

"Indeed," he said, his voice low in the noise, "she is weaving a living tapestry with herself and us in it as well as the King and the Lords of Eldwold. She has gone too far to stop, and so have I. She is no child: she has plotted this thing with me step by step and has kept it secret even from Coren. I am playing for power; it is a game my ancestors taught me, and I will play it until I die of it. Sybel is playing her own game of power, not for gain, or even for fame, but for a kind of dark triumph over Drede and even over Mithran. When she has had her triumph, she will come back to live quietly, contentedly with her animals and with Coren. It is not enough for me to know Sirle can defeat Drede—I must act in the knowledge, and keep acting afterward to protect my great power. But Sybel is more fortunate. She can achieve great power and then let it go and rest content in the knowledge of what she could do if she willed. If this were not true, I would be as frightened of her as Drede is. But there is love in her for Coren, for the children, for simple, quiet things. I think you taught her this, Maelga, when you loved her. Do not be worried. She will take her revenge and be satisfied."

Maelga watched him silently over her flickering jewels until he finished. Then she dropped her hands. "I could never talk to lions—I cannot growl. Where is she?"

"She may be with her animals. I will send for her."

"No." She rose. "Tell me how to find them. I will go there alone."

"I will take you and then leave you with her." He pushed his chair back, led her past the tables. "But if Coren is with her, talk of the weather, of star patterns, of how you ate nothing at the table of the Lord of Sirle. He is innocent of this; she values that."

They found her with Coren in the gardens, laughing together beside the lake while the Black Swan took bread pieces from Coren's fingers. The Cats lay lazily beneath the warm sun; Cyrin Boar nosed at something idly through the grass as he stood in the shade. Sybel turned as the gate closed behind Maelga. The smile on her face melted to astonishment.

"Maelga!"

Coren turned, tossed the rest of the bread into the water and followed Sybel, smiling as she flung her arms around Maelga.

"I am glad to see you."

"My white child, you have grown so—so bright! Let me look at you." She held Sybel at arm's length. "You did not stop to see me when you came to the Mountain last."

"How did you know—"

"Cyrin Boar told me. He told me many things."

Sybel's eyes grew still. She glanced at Coren, and he touched her cheek.

"I will go and let you talk."

She smiled. "Please, Coren. It is only women's talk."

"When one is a witch and the other a wizard, I doubt that." He left them. They looked at one another a moment, quietly. Then Maelga's fingers folded against one another and she brought them to her mouth.

"My child, what are you doing?"

Sybel sighed. "Sit down. How did you get here?"

"On my own feet."

"Oh, Maelga, you should have taken a horse."

"I was afraid whom I might steal from . . ." She got down beside Sybel, under a strong-limbed apple tree. "Cyrin told me a tale Ter had told him of a King and a white bird in a tower . . ."

Sybel glanced at the silver Boar. "Wisdom never learned silence, and it is most annoying when least wanted."

"Why did you not tell me what Drede did to you?"

Her mouth tightened. "Because it hurt too much. Because I was angry to my heart's core and there were no words for it. That little King would have—" She brushed her hand across the grass impatiently. "There are no words in either you or Cyrin to stop me."

"Sybel, I do not know what you are doing–I only know that Tam came to me two days ago—"

"Tam?"

"Afraid. He said war was murmuring all over Eldwold against his father, and the King blamed you. He said lords who had pledged to help his father suddenly turned to Sirle without reason. He said the King walks like a man of stone. Sybel, he sat at my hearth with his eyes wide, unblinking, while he told me this, and his hands gripping his arms as if he were cold. There were no tears left in him."

Sybel picked a single grass-blade, stared down at it

without seeing it. She shivered a little. "My poor Tam . . . It will only be a little while longer."

"And then what?"

"Then Drede will lose his throne. Perhaps his mind. Perhaps his life."

"And Tam?"

"Rok will make a king of him. In a suitable time he will marry Herne's daughter Vivet, and her sons will begin the Sirle line of Kings in Eldwold."

"And Coren? I have heard he knows nothing of this."

"Maelga, as I will do what I must to destroy Drede, I will do what I must to keep Coren from knowing what I am doing—"

"How? Will you destroy a thought or two in his mind?"

Her face twisted. She dropped her head on her bent knees, hidden from the searching gray eyes. "No," she whispered. "I will not do that. I did that once. Once. I will not do it again. I will lose him first. Maelga, I have taken a step in the dark, and I will not turn back for any word in Eldwold. I am glad to see you, but I think now you are not so glad to see me. I have been hurt, and now I will hurt in my own turn. It is that simple. I am sorry for Tam. But that is the only thing I am sorry for."

"You do not see," Maelga whispered. "Child, Tam loves that King. Drede is the one in the world who can look into Tam's eyes and give Tam his pride. And he is being driven mad before Tam's eyes."

"What is that to me?" She rose abruptly, facing the afternoon wind so that it blew her hair tangled, restless behind her. "He must find his own pride. Maelga —" She lifted her hands suddenly to her face and found tears slipping between her cold fingers. She covered her eyes with her fingers. "I cannot forgive him," she whispered. "My heart aches for Tam, but I cannot. I will not. And I will not cry for myself . . . only a little for Tam. Did he blame me himself?"

"He suspects that Drede did something to make you angry. But he does not believe—he does not want to believe that you could terrify Drede so, because you know he loves Drede. Oh, he sees things in his heart and he closes his heart's eye to them, a child closing his eyes to the dark. When he is forced to open his eyes, Sybel, what will you tell him? What comfort will you give him? His heart will shrink like a wounded thing from any touch."

"It is Drede's fault." She shook her head abruptly. "No. It is my doing, too. But Drede should never have tried to ruin me."

"He is doing it now."

Sybel turned, looked down at her, dark eyed. "That may be, but now it is my choice. Drede was a fool and so was Mithran, for underestimating that white-haired woman they caught. And neither of them will ever make that mistake again." She paused a moment, then said more gently. "I am hard and stubborn these days. There is no moving me. Maelga, let us talk of other things now, little things. I am sorry we did not stop to see you that night, but Drede's men found us there with Tam and it seemed wiser to leave without speaking to you, in case we were watched."

Maelga's hands moved in the long grass. Lines puckered her brow above her sharp eyes but she said only, "Are you happy, then, with the wise one of Sirle?"

"Yes. I want no one else, ever. I want to bear him children, if—if he wants them of me when this is done."

"You expect none yet?"

"No." She sat down again in the grass. "But perhaps it is better for the moment. I am happy here, Maelga. The people are good to me, and the children and women seem so bright, so contented among the gray stones. I miss the deep, roaring winds, the clear streams and the quiet places of Eld Mountain; the animals miss them, too, sometimes, but we are all content enough here among men. Rok made a room for me, high in the house with windows facing north, east and south, and he put my books there. I read there, and call. I miss you, too. I cannot run to you for comfort, though there is no one, these days, to give me comfort."

Maelga touched a strand of the white hair that brushed across her hand. "I miss you, too. But now I see the Lion was right: you are no longer a child. You have grown a queen among men. You no longer would be happy among the stones and trees of the Mountain. But I see the ghost of you sometimes, slipping barefoot through the great red pillars with a round-eyed child running at your side. And the shadows of you make me stop and smile. And then I remember they are only shadows, that my children have grown away from me, gone their ways . . ." She sighed, her lean hands fluttering. "But I was so fortunate to have you."

Sybel's fingers closed gently around Maelga's parchment-colored, ringed hand. "And I was that fortunate to have you," she said softly. "I was as wild and proud as any of my animals that day I walked through your door. Whatever gentleness I have, you and Tam taught me, and later, Coren. But I am still wild, proud as my father and my grandfather were, deep in me where the white bird lives free that no man can capture. It is that pride in me crying out for revenge—the pride in my knowledge and power. That same pride drove Myk away from men to the isolation of Eld Mountain to build his white hall and capture perfection. But because of you and Tam, I learned to love something beyond pure knowledge. And Coren taught me greatly of joy . . . I may not be so good at loving, Maelga, but it is my own fault—I have been rich in teachers."

"My white one," Maelga whispered, "when you disappeared that night from your hall, I knew I would never see you again, and there was such a sorrow in my withered heart. And today, again, there is that sorrow . . . you will step again into the night and when I see you again I will look into a stranger's eyes."

"Strange to you, but Maelga, I think I have never been less strange to myself as now. It is a terrible thing to say, but there is a triumph in me that I do not even have the sense to fear. It is as though in my thoughts I am Gyld, flying high, high in the night sky, huge, powerful, irresistible, with pride in all the memories of battles, of slayings, of stealings, of songs where my name is a beat of awe and fear. There is no one in all the world to check my night flight of triumph. When it is done, that thing in me will find a place to coil and sleep and I can forget it."

"But will you forget? Rok will ask more of you, and more— I saw that in his Lion's eyes. And Tam—you may teach Tam to ask of you—"

"No. Tam is good. And Rok will spare me for Coren's sake."

"Will he? Will you even care by then for Coren's love?"

"I will care. I care now."

"But you fly alone, away from him— I wonder, will you want to come back earthward after that flight?"

Sybel sighed. She loosed Maelga's hand and touched her eyes with her fingers. "I am tired of the ceaseless weave to and fro of questioning, wondering, thinking. I will set Eldwold aflame and then find out if I am trapped within the ring of fire, or safe outside it . . . Maelga, you must be tired, too, after your long walk. Let me take you to my chamber, where you can eat, and wash and rest."

"I will not rest in this house."

"Well. Then if you will not stay here with me, let Rok send someone with you to Herne's house, or Bor's house."

Maelga patted Sybel's hand. She rose a little unsteadily and brushed the grass off her skirt. "No. I will rest here a while, with your animals. I will go and sit with the Black Swan. Such a lovely swan fountain, there. I never cared much for men's houses—you cannot get in and out of them easily."

Sybel smiled a little. "No." She put her arm around Maelga, walked with her to the lake. The Black Swan glided to meet them. "I will bring you food and wine. If you want to sleep out here tonight, I will stay with you."

Maelga sank down at the lake's edge. "Oh, my bones. The sun is so kind in summer to an old woman. And you are kind, still, to powerless things. It is comforting."

"I will be back soon," Sybel said.

"There is no hurry, my white one. I will take a little nap." She closed her eyes. Sybel went quietly to the gate, closed it softly behind her as she left. Then she looked up to see Coren standing before her, and she blinked, startled.

"Oh—"

He lifted his hands slowly, gripped her arms. His eyes moved back and forth across her face, narrowed, bewildered, as though he were reading ancient words he could not understand. Then he drew a breath and shouted,

"Sybel, what are you doing?"

ELEVEN

Her heart grew withered and chill within her, slowing the startled leap of her blood. She lifted a finger to her lips, feeling the beat of her heart in her mouth, her throat dry as powdered earth. "Be quiet, Coren. Maelga is sleeping."

"Sybel!"

"Let me go. I will not lie to you."

His hands loosened slowly, fell clenched to his sides. He stared down at her, sun streaking his eyes, the blood high beneath his skin. He said slowly, distinctly,

"I went—"

"Sh—"

"I have been still too long! I went to the stables, and Ceneth and Bor were there, and Bor was saddling his horse to ride back to his house; I heard your name on their lips, and your name again—they laughed, saying how you drew the old Lord of Hilt like a child to Rok's hall. I stood there as they laughed, and I felt as though —as though they had struck me and laughed—there was a sickness in me, and—then they saw me, because —a sound had come out of me, and the laughter left them like flame blown out."

"Coren—" she whispered.

"Sybel, why? Why? Why am I the first man to know every outward part of you and the last of all men to know your inward mind? Why did Rok, Ceneth and Bor know, and not me? Why did you not tell me what you are doing? Why did you lie to me?"

"Because I did not want you to look at me the way you are looking now—"

"Sybel, that is no kind of reason!"

"Stop shouting at me!" she flared suddenly. She caught her breath and pressed her cold hands briefly against her eyes. She felt his nearness, his taut stillness, heard in the moment's darkness the deep beat of his breathing.

"All right," he whispered. "I will not shout. You healed me once when I might have died, and now you had better do it again because there is a thing in me that is hurt and sick. I am beginning to wonder, Sybel, why you chose to marry me at all, and so suddenly at that, after your dark night away, and what great anger you have against Drede that you would stir Sirle against him. Sybel, my thoughts are pounding against my brain —I cannot still them. Do not lie to me anymore."

Her hands slipped from her eyes, and they were dusted with a bloom of weariness. "Drede paid Mithran to capture me and destroy my mind."

A sound came inarticulate from him. "Drede? Drede?"

She nodded. "Drede wanted to marry me and use me without fear. Rommalb killed Mithran, crushing him. And I will crush Drede with his own fears, take his power from him through Sirle. I used our marriage to frighten Drede; I planned from the beginning to use my powers for Sirle against him. I did not tell you all this because my revenge is my own affair, not yours, and I did not want to hurt you with the knowledge that I had used you. Now you know and you are hurt, and I do not think this time I can heal your wounds."

He stared at her. His head turned a little, as though he were trying to catch a faint sound lost in the wind. His words came finally in a hollow whisper, "I do not know, either—Ice-white Lady, I think I hold you in my hands and then you melt and slip cold through my fingers . . . How could you hurt me like this? How could you?"

Her face crumpled. Hot tears gathered in his eyes and he wavered, glittering before her. "I tried so to keep you from knowing—to keep you from being hurt—"

"Did you really care? Or am I just one more in your collection of strange, wondrous beasts to be used at your need, to be put aside while you go about your business?"

"Coren—"

"I could kill Rok for this, and Ceneth and Bor, but if I blasted all of Eldwold from the earth there would still be that blind fool in me who will mock me until I die. I love you. I love you so much. I would have torn Drede apart for you with my hands, if only you had told me he had hurt you. Why did you not tell me? I would have plotted a war for you such as Eldwold has never seen."

"Coren—I could not tell you— I could not drag you into my hate and rage— I did not want you to know how—how cold and terrible I can be—"

"Or how little you need me?"

"I need you—"

"You need Rok and Ceneth more than you need me. Sybel, I do not understand this game you are playing. Do you think if I know you, I will fear you? Cease to love you?"

"Yes," she whispered. "As you are doing now."

He gripped her suddenly, shook her, hurting her. "That is not true! What do you think love is—a thing to startle from the heart like a bird at every shout or blow? You can fly from me, high as you choose into your darkness, but you will see me always beneath you, no matter how far away, with my face turned to you. My heart is in your heart. I gave it to you with my name that night and you are its guardian, to treasure it, or let it wither and die. I do not understand you. I am angry with you. I am hurt and helpless, but nothing would fill the ache of the hollowness in me where your name would echo if I lost you." He loosed her. She watched him, wide-eyed, her hair drifting across her face. He turned away from her suddenly. She reached out to him.

"Where are you going?"

"To find the Lion of Sirle."

She went with him, hurrying to keep up with his swift, furious strides. They found Rok at a table in the empty hall, with Ceneth sitting hunched beside him, a cup in his hand. Rok watched Coren, his eyes brilliant, chill-blue in his flushed face, come toward him unmoved; when Coren's fists pounded sharply on the wood in front of him, and Ceneth jumped, Rok said simply,

"I know."

"If you know, then why? Then why?"

"You must know why." He paused a moment. A weariness loosened his smooth voice. "A woman came to me and offered me money and power for the destruction of the man who killed Norrel, who sent Sirle to its knees at Terbrec. I did not think of her; I did not think of you. I simply accepted what I have wanted, day and night, for thirteen years. I have done what I have done. What will you do now? You, too, have wanted this war."

"Not this way!"

"War is war. What is it you want, Coren? To let Drede go unpunished for the wrong he has done your wife?"

Coren's fists shifted, taut, shaking, on the table. "I would have gone to Mondor alone, unarmed, to kill him with my bare hands if she had told me then. But she went to you. And now I stand a man outside a circle of secrecy, looking into it for the first time, not knowing how to name what I see. Where are your eyes, Rok of Sirle? Could you not see that step by step, moment by moment, you were watching my wife destroy herself in lies, in bitterness, in hatred? And you watched her with your calm eyes and said nothing! Nothing! You used her as she used you; now what is left in either of you? I know that endless road she has taken—you know it, too. Yet you did not lift a hand to stop her, did not drop one word to me so I could!"

Rok lifted a hand, drew his fingers wearily across his eyes. Ceneth, hunched over his wine, lifted his head.

"What are you going to do, Coren? You could kill us all—except Herne and Eorth; they knew nothing. Or you could refuse to fight. Or you could try to forget that your pride is hurt, accept what is inevitable—"

"Is it inevitable?" He straightened, turned so suddenly that Sybel started. He looked at her out of stranger's eyes. "Is it?"

Her shoulders slumped wearily. "Coren. I love you. But I cannot stop this thing."

He gripped her. Sybel," he whispered. "Once—I gave up for you something like this—gave up a dream of revenge, a nightmare of grief that was like a long sickness. Now I will ask you. Give this thing up. If not for me, then for Tam."

She looked at him. "Please," she whispered. His hands slid slowly away from her, dropped.

"You want it that badly. So. You have learned what you were afraid Tam would learn—the taste of power. Well, I will give you your war. But I do not know what you will have left when it is over."

He turned and left them. Sybel watched him move

away from her wordlessly. When she could not see him, she moved to the table, sat down abruptly. The two men watched her, waited for her to cry. When she simply sat unmoving, Ceneth poured wine, pushed the cup to her. She touched it without drinking, her eyes empty. At last she took a sip that stirred a faint color in her face. Ceneth ran his hands through his black hair.

"I am sorry. I am so sorry. To babble it all in the stable like a pair of children—I have seen a man wounded with that look on his face, but never a man standing healthy on his two feet. What woman alive does not scheme a little behind her husband's back?"

"So I am like any other woman. That is comforting, but Coren is not like any other man." She pressed her cold fingers a moment against her eyes. "I do not want to talk of it. Please. Let us make a swift end to all this. When will Derth of Niccon be ready with his boats?"

"In a week perhaps. He needs time to gather his men."

She drew a breath, loosed it. "Well. Then I will have to learn to look into Coren's eyes. I suppose I should be thankful I do not have to look into Tam's."

Rok reached across the table, held her hand. "We could finish without you, now that we have Hilt and Niccon."

"No." She smiled a little, her eyes black, mirthless. "No. I still have a King to catch. We are going to suffer together, Drede and I . . . and afterward—I do not know." Her head bowed, dropped onto her outstretched arm. "I do not know," she whispered.

"Sybel. He will forgive you. He will realize how terribly you were used, and he will forgive you."

"The only thing he has to forgive her for," Ceneth said, "is not allowing him to be angry with Drede himself, to revenge his own wife."

She made a sudden, impatient gesture. "I did not

marry him because he had a swift temper and a restless sword."

"But, Sybel, if he loves you, he expects to know these things. You hurt his pride badly."

"I hurt deeper than that. He thinks I do not love him. Which may be so. I do not know. I do not know anymore what love is. I am merciless to those two I love most, Tam and Coren, and I cannot stop this thing for their sakes . . . it must drag on and on, heavy and wearisome, until it comes to an irreversible end."

"He loves you deeply," Rok said gently, "and you will have long years afterward to learn to live with one another."

"Or without." She stirred restlessly. "I came for some food for Maelga. She will not come in the house, but she is resting in the gardens." She rose. She stood a moment in silence, her face colorless, her hand taut on the table as though she could not move. Rok touched her, and she looked down at him as though she had forgotten him.

"You are not terrible," he said softly, "and I think you do love him, or you would not be so grieved. Be patient. It will soon be over."

"Soon is such a long word," she whispered.

She went down to the kitchens, took soft bread, fresh cheeses, fruit, meat and wine for Maelga, and carried them to the garden. She stopped before the open gate, looked through the trees, but saw only the great Cats playing a silent, sinuous game, and Cyrin Boar sleeping in the sunlight. She caught the mind of the Black Swan.

Where is Maelga?

Sybel, the witch woke and left, the Swan answered. *She said the world was too large for her.*

Sybel's brows tugged together anxiously. She went to Cyrin, woke him.

Did Maelga say why she left?

No, said the Boar. *But when the Lord of Dorn entered the dark house of the Riddle Master, he—*

"I know, I know." She finished wearily, "He ate neither food nor wine, nor did he sleep through the night—Cyrin, Rok's food is quite harmless." She stared down at the food until it seemed like something unfamiliar, of another world. Then, wielding the tray with both hands, she wheeled and flung it through the trees, so that grape, meat and bread fell through the leaves in a soft shower, and the heavy silver tray traced an arc of slow-turning circles in the air and fell ringing on its side beside the Cats. They stared at her, surprised motionless at their play. She stared back at them a moment, almost as startled. Then she whirled and left.

Sybel sat at her window, embroidering a battle design on Coren's cloak, watching the slow gathering of night above the Sirle forests. She saw Coren at last, riding across the fields, dark beneath the blue-black sky; heard, in the quiet air, his faint shout to the gatehouse, and the boom of the lowered bridge. Later, she heard his steps in the hall. Her hands stilled, dropped in her lap; her face turned toward the closed door. He opened it, paused a little when he saw her. Then he came in, closed the door.

"Why are you not at supper?"

"I could not eat." She watched him pour wine. "Where did you go?"

"To Mirkon Forest. I sat tossing a stone in my hand and learned nothing at all from it. Wine?"

"Please."

He brought her a cup, sat beside her on the window seat. She watched him drink; his face was quiet, colorless in the candlelight. He lowered his cup and touched a fold of the cloak.

"There are still things I am unsure of, in this war of yours and Rok's. You must have brought the Lord of

Niccon here, too—he never would have come otherwise."

"Yes." Something leaped then in her throat; she swallowed dryly. "And—there is something else, in the way of truth, that I must tell you."

He looked at her, his eyes apprehensive, but he said only, "Tell me."

"You saw—you might have guessed that day Derth came, what we were doing—you questioned Rok after he had lied to you about Eorth riding Gyld, and—I saw the doubt in your eyes when you looked at me."

"I do not remember."

"You do not remember because I—made you forget."

"You what?"

"I went into your mind. I found those memories and took them and then it was as though it never happened." He was still then, his breath still. "I told you so—so that you will know that it happened once, and will never happen again."

"I see," he whispered. He lifted the cup to his mouth; it shook slightly in his hand. He placed it on the stones between them. "I never thought you would do that to me. I never thought you would want to."

"That—that is why I came running to you, crying. Because I had done that thing to you that Drede and Mithran would have done to me. I was afraid then of myself. But when you took me in your arms and held me, I felt—if you loved me, I could not be what I glimpsed myself to be. But now, I have no one to tell me not to be afraid. What do you see now, when you look at me?"

"Something of a stranger in your dark eyes." He leaned forward; she felt his fingers lightly touch her face, as he said with a wistfulness that ached in her, "Where is the woman who lay so quietly in my arms that night on Eld Mountain?"

"I am sorry," she whispered. "I am sorry I married you."

His hand closed, dropped on the stones. "I was afraid of hearing that." His eyes closed. "So what shall I do now? I cannot stop loving you."

"Coren, I do not want you to. Only—I will hurt you as I will hurt Tam. And I think when this is done, neither of you will forgive me."

"Tam. What is to become of him in your plans? That child of yours who loved red foxes."

"We are going to make a king of him, ruled by the Sirle Lords. And one day he will look at me and see a stranger, too."

"And Drede. Sybel, what are you planning to do with him?"

"I will deal with whatever is left of him afterward. I do not care about his death, only about his life, and he is so frightened now of me that he is nearly mad—" She checked, looking up at him as he rose, his eyes wide, incredulous.

"Sybel, how can you—how can you drive him and me mad so coldly—"

"I am not cold! You have hated, yourself—you told me! How did your blood run, Coren? thick and hot in your heart? How did you hate? Did you nurse revenge from a tiny, moon-pale seedling in the night places in your heart, watch it grow and flower and bear dark fruit that hung ripe—ripe for the plucking? It becomes a great, twisted thing of dark leaves and thick, winding vines that chokes and withers whatever good things grow in your heart; it feeds on all the hatred your heart can bear— That is what is in me, Coren. Not all the wondrous joy and love of you can wither that night plant in me. I have plotted revenge from the night I came out to you at Maelga's house with my torn dress open so that you could look at me and want me as Mithran wanted me—"

She heard the sharp hiss of breath between his teeth. Then he struck her, a sudden, open-handed blow across the mouth that shocked her silent.

"I was no more than that to you! No more than Mithran!"

She lifted her fingers to her face. "No one has ever hit me before," she said. He stared down at her stillness and an incoherent keen broke from him.

"You do not even care. Oh, White Lady, now what shall I do? he whispered. "I do not know what to do."

He turned from her blindly; she saw his hands grope over the door, open it. She dropped her head on her knees, hiding her face in the folds of his cloak, but she saw his agony even behind the darkness of her closed eyes.

She finished the cloak for him, the deep blue cloth blazoned with the snow-white falcon of the Sirle Lords, and word came from Niccon on the day she finished it that the boats were finished and had been sent downriver from a branch of the Slinoon that fed from the Lake of the Lost King on the northern borders of Niccon. Rok called his brothers to the house, and Sybel sat with them, listening quietly beside Coren.

"We will meet Derth of Niccon in two days at the point where Edge River meets the Slinoon," Rok said. "Horst of Hilt will meet us at Mondor, coming from the east. He will have to break through the forces of the men on his land who are fighting for Drede, so Eorth and Bor, you will lead half of our men to close in behind those forces, crush them between you and Horst's army. We will occupy Drede at Mondor; his army is guarding the Slinoon up from the city a little. We will drive him back toward Mondor. Ceneth, you and Herne will lead the men downriver, into the city to take Drede's stronghold, and to—" He paused at a movement from Coren.

"Let me go instead of Herne."

"I want you with me."

"I want," Coren said, "to go instead of Herne. Herne is a great fighter, but he does not think. I think. And walking alive into the heart of Drede's city will require thought."

Rok sighed. "It is a gift," he said bluntly, "to Sybel. You will go with me."

"I will go with Ceneth or not at all. I am thinking of Tamlorn. What is to stop some great warrior, hot with bloodletting, from taking the life of one defenseless boy whose crime it was to be Drede's son?"

"Ter will be with him," Sybel said. He turned to her, and she saw again, as she had been seeing through the past days, the clear line of bone beneath the skin of his face, the curved lines beneath his eyes.

"Do you want me with Rok?"

She shook her head, her hands folded tight on the table. "Do what you must. But is it Tam you want to save? Or do you want to challenge death, ask it a riddle?"

She saw his teeth come together in his closed mouth. "You have a third eye, Sybel. But the pride in me will not let me stay behind with Rok. If I meet Drede and give you his head on my sword point, will that satisfy you?"

Her voice shook. "No."

"What gift will, then?"

"Coren, let it be," Ceneth murmured. "You may hate us all, but we have a battle before us, and whether you fight for us or against us or not at all, make the choice and keep it."

"Oh, I will fight with you," Coren said. "But I will not stay safe with Rok while you and Herne whet your swords on Drede's hearthstones." He turned back to Rok. "There is a young boy I know who once ran barefoot on Eld Mountain, and who will lose his father in this war, who will see his father's guards slain before his eyes, who will have only a Falcon at his side that cannot tell him he will live to be King of Eldwold. He gave me my life once. Let me spare him some terror. Let me do at least that for him."

Rok looked at Sybel, but her eyes were hidden, and her folded hands against her mouth. He said finally, "You and Ceneth will lead men of your own choice into the city. Ter will tell Sybel where Tam is, and she will tell Coren."

"No," Sybel said. Her hands dropped. "I will not go into Coren's mind. When Ter flies out to you, you will know Tam is near. If his life is in danger, though, he will be taken by the Swan to Eld Mountain."

"But if Drede hides him," Ceneth said, "how will we know where to look for him? You could tell Coren—slip the knowledge in his mind—"

"No."

Ceneth sighed. "Then tell me, and I will tell Coren. You have done so much mind work already that—"

"Ceneth," Rok said wearily, "be quiet."

"But I think—"

"Do you?" Coren said, and his question snapped in the air like breaking ice. Ceneth flushed under his gaze.

"I am quiet," he breathed. "But I am wondering who exactly you are fighting in this war."

Eorth's broad hand dropped onto the table. "Ceneth, be quiet," he begged. "I have forgotten half of what Rok has said already. If we are going to get this war off the table and into the field, you will all have to stop bickering."

"That," Bor grunted, "is the wisest thing you have ever said."

Sybel closed her eyes with her fingers. "If Tam is in any great danger I will see to it you know. One thing I must warn you: you may see strange, wonderful beasts on the battlefield, if you are close-pressed with

Drede's men. Do not follow them. Oh, you have seen them here, but in the magic of their luring they grow oddly beautiful. I have told them to stay away from you, but warn your own men, or they may wake to themselves lost in some quiet forest."

A sudden smile broke over Herne's lean, restless face. "This will be a war for harpists to break their strings over for centuries."

"Yes," Eorth said, "but first I have to know again what was going on before the animals came in."

Rok refilled his cup and began the weave again patiently.

Twilight closed over the hundred eyes of fires ringing the Sirle house. Sybel, leaving the rest of the planning to the warlords under Rok's command, watched the fires' patternless flickering from her high window. Coren came in eventually as the night deepened. She rested her face against the cold stones, listening to the sound of his undressing. She heard the rustle of cloth against cloth drawn back, the whisper of his breath across candle flame. She drew off her clothes, slipped into bed beside him. She lay awake, knowing from his restless breathing his own wakefulness. The night wind stirred between them, traced her cheek with a cold finger. She heard his breathing deepen finally; she lay awake long, watching the curve of his arm and side change and fall with his breathing in the faint moonlight. Then she turned away from him, one hand over her eyes, and thought of Drede lying awake among his own stones, watching the torch flame wash across his walls. Coren stirred, disturbing her thoughts. He quieted, then shifted again with a little, sharp cry. She felt then, in the quiet darkness, a shadow over her own thoughts, as though she were watched, secretly. She turned abruptly.

The Blammor stood over her. She had no time to cry out before the crystal eyes met hers, aloof as stars, and then the darkness overwhelmed her and she heard all around her the thick, imperative beat of her own heart. Visions ran through her mind, of a wizard lying broken on his rich skins, of the death faces of men through the ages meeting the core of their nightmares one final time in rooms without windows, between stone walls without passage. A wet air hovered with the darkness, carrying the cloying scent of pooled blood, of wet, rusted iron; she tasted dry, powdered dust, the withered leaves of dying trees, heard the faint, last cries like a dark wind from some ancient battlefield, of pain, of terror, of despair. And then her thoughts lifted away from her into some plane of terror she had never known, and she struggled blindly, drowning in it.

A vision hovered white as the Blammor's eye somewhere beneath the terror. While a part of her cried helpless, voiceless against the welling darkness, a thought, trained, honed to a fine perception, detached itself, probed toward the misty image. It lay drifting at the bottom of her mind; she searched for it as though calling through the deepest places of Eldwold, and finally, beneath her mind's eye, the image clarified and she found a moon-white bird with twisted trailing wings, lying broken, the curve of its smooth neck snapped back against itself.

She whispered, "No." And then she found herself on the floor, her face against the stones, her breath coming in whimpering, shuddering gasps. She lifted her head, felt tears drying on her face in the cool air. Then she felt the darkness full around her of a looming Thing that watched, waited. She drew herself up, shaking, weak. She stepped toward Coren, but he lay a stranger, as though he were in a dream beyond her. She stood motionless, looking at him, until her trembling eased. And then soundlessly she dressed.

She made her way through the winding stone corridor, slipped like a shadow past the guarded hall, past the inner wall where the slow steps of men paced back and forth above her head. She opened the gate to the gardens, held it wide in the moonlight, and the whisperings came to her of animals wakened, moving toward her in the night. She saw the great shape of Gules Lyon first, and she reached out to him, clung to his mane.

What is it, White One?

I am going back to Eld Mountain. You are free.

Free?

The Black Cat Moriah brushed against her. She looked deep into the green eyes.

You must do what you will tomorrow. I ask nothing of you. Nothing. You are free.

But what of you, Sybel? What of Drede?

I cannot—there is a price for his death I cannot pay.

Sybel, said the flute-voiced Swan, *free to fly the gray autumn sky once more? Free to taste the wind on the wing tip?*

Yes.

But what of Tam?

I will ask nothing of you. Nothing. You must do as you will.

She touched Gyld's mind, found him awake, with slow thoughts revolving in his mind of a wet-walled cave deep in a silent mountain, with a tiny stream in it that trickled across pieces of gold and pale bone.

You are free.

But what of Drede? Shall I slay him for you first?

I do not want to hear his name again! I do not care if he lives or dies, if he wins or loses this war—I do not care! You are free.

Free. The various voices brushed in her mind like the sounds of instruments.

Free from the winter . . . free to run gold as the sun beneath the desert sun's eye.

Free to fly to the world's edge on the rim of twilight. Free to be stroked by fat-fingered kings in the Southern Deserts, to hear the whisperings of moon-eyed witches.

Free to dream in the silence of one treasure greater than them all.

Free, said the silver-bristled Boar. *Answer me a riddle, Sybel. What has set you free?*

She stared into his red eyes. *You know. You know. My eyes turned inward and I looked. I am not free. I am small and frightened, and darkness runs at my heels, in my running, watches.*

Sybel, said the Black Swan, *I will take you to Eld Mountain. And then I will fly to the lakes beyond North Eldwold that lie like the scattered jewels of sleeping queens.*

I will take you, Gyld said. *And then I will wind my path again deep, deep into my sweet cave.*

Take me then, she said, and felt his lumbering movements in the cave. She bent down, held Gules Lyon's mane, looked deep into his eyes.

"Gules," she whispered, and felt his mind drift away from hers, leaving the memories of him like things shadowed in a dim room. She loosed him and he left her, running huge and silent across the Sirle fields. She turned to the Cat.

"Moriah."

The great Cat slipped, shadow-dark, into the shadows, its green eyes winking back at the moon.

"Black Swan," she whispered, and it rose above her, circling slow, the great span of its wings black against the moon, curving to a line of breathless wonder.

"Cyrin."

The marble-tusked Boar stood a moment before her. "The Riddle Master himself lost the key to his own riddles one day," he said in his deep, reed-pure voice, "and he found it again at the bottom of his heart. Farewell, Sybel. The Lord of Dorn ran three times around the doorless walls of the house of the witch Enyth, and then walked into the wall and it vanished like a dream."

"Farewell," she whispered. He ran out of the open gate, moon-bright across the fields of sleeping men. She straightened, called Ter from his post beside the sleeping Tam in the stone walls of Mondor.

Ter. You are free.

No.

Ter. You are free to do as you will, to go from Tam or to stay with him, king's bird. But one thing I ask of you. One thing for my sake. Do not touch Drede. He is mine and I choose to forget him.

But why, Ogam's child? Where is your triumph?

Gone, in the night. I have awakened, alone and afraid.

Afraid?

Afraid, fearless one. You are free.

She whispered his name, and it fell without answer in the still night. She rose, mounted the green-winged Dragon. She rode high with him through the star-flecked night, high above the war fires of Sirle, of Mondor, to a high mountain and a white hall of silence, where she loosed the Dragon forever from her. She went into the doors of Myk's cold, empty house and locked them behind her.

TWELVE

Seven days later the King of Eldwold rode with his guards up the winding path of Eld Mountain. He rode past the tiny house of the witch of Maelga, with the doves in its yard and the black raven on the worn stag's antlers above the door. He stopped at the closed gates of the wizard's white hall, and saw through them the motionless, tangled garden, the covering of pine needles across the stone path between the gate and the closed door. A breath of wind stirred pale strands of his hair across his face. He brushed them aside and dismounted.

"Wait here for me."

"Lord, she is dangerous—"

His face turned abruptly upward, the bones of it forming sharp beneath his skin. "She would never hurt me. Wait here."

"Yes, Lord."

He tried the iron railings of the gate with his hands, but they were shut fast. He stared at them a moment, his brows knit over his eyes. Then he wedged one foot into a high crevice in the stone wall, gripped the jutting stones with his hands, pulled himself up. Cloth of his black tunic ripped against a sharp finger of rock; he loosed himself absently and found another foothold, and another, until his hands closed, splayed and bloodless, on the smooth molding of marble on top of the wall. He swung a leg over and dropped on his knees onto the soft earth below.

He rose and dusted his stockings. The wind fell, leaving the gardens silent. His eyes searched, narrowed, puzzled through the dark shadows of underleaves, through the smooth, sun-rich trunks of great pine, but no movement answered his moving eyes. He went down the walk slowly, and turned the door latch. He shook the door slightly, knocked on it. One of the guards called hopefully from beyond the gate,

"Perhaps, Lord, she is not there."

He did not answer. The windows of the house stared blindly outward, like eyes without a flicker of thought behind them. He stepped back a little, his lips between his teeth. Then he bent swiftly and picked up a smooth stone beside the path. He tapped it gently against a diamond of thick glass in a window and it cracked into a web of a thousand lines, then fell showering to the inner floor. He picked out teeth of glass still clinging to the rim, then slid his arm through to the elbow and groped for the window latch.

"Lord, be careful!"

The window opened abruptly; he swung with it sideways against the white wall. He drew his arm back. Within, dust drifted in the placid sunlight to the floor. He blinked into the dimness, listening for any sound, but the rooms were still as though no one walked or breathed in them. He heaved himself up, his feet slipping against the smooth marble and brought a knee over the ledge.

"Sybel?"

The word hung in the sunlight with the golden, dancing specks of dust. He turned his body, swung from the window onto the floor. He rose and walked through the silence to the great domed room beyond and saw the moon-pure crystal of it arched pale above him. And then he saw beneath it, sitting in white silence, a woman with hair the color of sun-touched frost sitting still, as though cased in ice. Her black eyes were open, blind.

He went forward, his steps soundless on the thick fur. He knelt before her, looked into her eyes.

"Sybel?"

He touched her lightly, hesitantly, his brows crooked. The white face, the bones clear beneath it, seemed formed of stone, so still, so secret. The slender hands, the bones outlined at every curve and joint, folded motionless. He stared at her, his own hands moving flat, restless, up and down his thighs, and a little, incoherent sound came out of his throat. He drew breath again and shouted suddenly,

"Sybel!"

She started, stirred faintly, and a little color came into her face. Her eyes focused on his face, and he smiled, wordless with relief. She leaned forward, one hand moving slowly out of the sheath of her hair to touch him.

"Tam . . ."

He nodded jerkily. "Yes—" Her hand touched his mouth, wandered across one shoulder. Then it dropped. Her eyes dropped; she drew a long, endless breath. Her face bowed until he could scarcely see it. He reached out, drew her hair back.

"Sybel, please. Please. Do not go back where you were. Please. Talk to me. Say my name."

She covered her eyes with her fingers. "Tam."

"No. I am not Tam anymore. I am Tamlorn. Sybel, I am Tamlorn, King of Eldwold."

She saw him then clearly, his hands gripping his bent knees, his pale hair neatly trimmed, capping his lean, brown face. She saw the tense set and play of his mouth, the shadows beneath his eyes and the bones beneath his skin. The rich black tunic he wore caught the color from his eyes, darkening them. She stirred, feeling stiffness in every joint and bone.

"Why did you bring me back?"

"Where did you go? Sybel, why? Why?"

"I had no place else to go."

"Sybel, you are so thin. They said you were not in Sirle, and I had to find you, to ask you something. So I came here, and your gates were locked. So I climbed the wall, but your door was locked. So I broke a window and climbed in and found you, but I could not reach inside you. You sat so still, as though you were made of stone and your eyes stared at me without seeing. Sybel, why did you go? Was it—what my father did to you?"

"It was what I did to myself."

His head moved briefly as if flicking away her answer. He reached out, touching her hair again, drawing with light, eager touches strand after strand of hair away from her face.

"My father told me what he did to you."

"He told—"

"Yes. The night before the fighting started. He told —he told me. Sybel, he was so frightened of you, he— I did not even know him, those days before the war. Then, when he told me why, I understood." He paused a moment, and a muscle beside his mouth jerked and was still. His eyes came back to her face. "Sybel, he said he came back to the tower to get you that day, and the door was wide open to the wizard's room and he went in and you were gone and—the wizard lay dead on the floor with his eyes—torn and every bone in him broken. And then he began to be afraid. And then you married Coren of Sirle . . . He rarely spoke after that, except to give orders, to consult with people.

He seldom spoke to me, but sometimes, when he sat alone in his rooms, with all the torches lit, just sitting, staring at nothing, I would go and sit with him, silently because I knew—I knew he wanted me with him. He would never speak to me, but sometimes he would put his hand on my hair, or my shoulder, for a moment, quietly. Sybel. I loved him. But somehow, when I heard what he had done to you, I was not surprised, because I knew that you were angry with him for something that was his fault. It was too late to be surprised. and that—that night he died."

His hands dropped away from her. She watched his face, the color running again beneath her skin. "My Tam," she said finally, "what did he die of?"

He drew a breath and looked at her. "Sybel, I know you did not kill that wizard. I do not know how he died, but I think—I think what killed him killed Drede."

She shivered. "So," she whispered, "it walked that night in more places than Coren's house."

"Who? Sybel, did you see it, too?" She did not answer; he shifted, his hands curved taut around his knees. His voice broke. "Sybel, please! I have to ask you. Drede lay on the floor and there was not a wound on him anywhere, but I saw the look on his face before they hid him from me. They said his heart failed, but I think he died of terror."

A murmur came from her. She shifted, let her head fall on one raised knee. "My Tam, I am sorry."

"Sybel, what did he see before he died? What killed him?"

She sighed. "Tam, that wizard, and that King, and I all saw the same thing. Those two are dead, but I am alive, though I have been so far from myself I did not think anything would bring me back. I have been beyond the rim of my mind. It is a kind of running away. I cannot tell you what that Thing is; I only know that when Drede looked at it, he saw what was in himself and that destroyed him. I know that because I nearly destroyed myself."

He was silent a moment, struggling. He said finally, "But you had a right to be angry."

"Yes. But not to hurt those I love, or myself." She reached out, touched his face gently. "It is so good to hear you say my name again. I thought—I was certain you would be angry with me for what I have done to you."

"You did nothing."

"I put you like a defenseless pawn in the hands of Sirle. That my running could not stop."

He shook his head slightly, bewilderedly. "Sybel, I am not in Rok's hands. I have a few advisers, but there is no regent. Drede's cousin Margor was to rule until I turned sixteen if Drede died, but he disappeared. So did my father's warlords. So did Horst of Hilt, Derth of Niccon, his brother and their warlords. So did the six of Sirle and their warlords—"

She reached out to him, her lips parted. "Tam, what happened to them? Were they killed in battle?"

"Sybel, you know what happened. You must know. In the camp above Mondor where my father would have been, it was Gules who came and the few that saw him who did not follow him came back without words in them to describe the gold of him and his mane like thread upon thread of silk and his eyes that flashed like the sun. There was a harpist-warrior who made a song already of the sight of Gules bounding before twenty unarmed warlords across the Slinoon River, just as the dawn sun rose—and I have heard a song of Moriah who came to my Uncle Sehan's camp in West Hilt, and how a song came from her sweeter than a woman's singing from a velvet-curtained window—Sybel, you knew!"

"No. No, I did not know." She rose suddenly, her

hands against her mouth. "I set them free that night."

He stared up at her incredulously. "Why?"

"Because—I had betrayed them. And what song has come out of Sirle? One of Cyrin?"

He nodded. "They say the six brothers of Sirle and their warlords went boar hunting in Mirkon Forest instead of to battle. And Gyld—he terrified everyone. Some battles started between Horst's men and my uncle's in Hilt, and Gyld swept through them and there were men with broken backs and others burned. And everyone ran. I never saw Gyld breathe fire before. He flew over Mondor, and the boats that were coming into the city—there were only a handful that came without orders, wanting to loot Drede's house, and Gyld set fire to their boats and they swam ashore—those who had no heavy armor. And the people in the city stayed indoors for fear of Gyld, and I stayed guarded until I whispered to Ter that I wanted to go out and he drove the guards away for me. So I saw Gyld flying gold-green above Mondor, and then Ter flew away and my Aunt Illa sent people to get me. And in Niccon, the Lord of Niccon laid down his sword and so did his friend Thone of Perl, and his warlords in council with him and they followed the song of a Swan that the Niccon harpists say was like the murmur of love on a warm summer day when the bees are singing... Sybel, you did not—you did not tell them to do that?"

"I set them free to do as they willed... My Tam, I would have played a terrible game with you, making a shadow king of you ruled by Sirle..." She drew her hands wearily over her face. "I do not know what you have brought me back to. My animals are gone, I have lost Coren, I have lost myself—but still, the sound of your voice and your smile are good to know again..."

Tam rose. He put his arms around her tightly, his cheek against her hair. "Sybel, I need you still. I need to know you are here. I have many people who know my name, but only one or two or three that know who it belongs to. You did not do any terrible thing to me —and even if you had, I would still have loved you because I need to love you."

"My Tam, you are a child—" she whispered. He drew back, and she took his face between her hands. He smiled a little, quiet smile that touched his gray eyes like sun through a mist.

"Yes. So do not go away again. I lost Drede, and I do not want to lose you, too. I am a child because I did not care what either of you did, only that I loved you."

He loosed her. The late sun spilled through the dome, turned the white fur fiery at their feet. "Sybel, you are so thin. I think you should eat something."

"You are thin, too, my Tam. You have been troubled."

"Yes. But also, I am growing." He led her out of the domed room to the hearth. She sat down in a chair before the empty grate; he balanced on the arm of the other chair, looking down at her. "Does Maelga know you are here?"

"I do not know. If she came, I did not hear her."

"You locked yourself in. But anyone who really wanted to could get in. Sybel, I think we should go to Maelga's house and let her fix us some supper."

A smile touched her face, smoothing the sharp lines of it. "I think you are wise, my Tam. I have lost everything, and you are a young King in a perilous position, whose valuable advisers and counselors are running in circles after wondrous animals in dark forests, and I do not know what tomorrow will bring either one of us, but today I am hungry and I think we must be fed."

They went, the silvery-haired wizard woman and the boy king, through the tall whispering trees and above them as they walked, the mists rolled again over the white face of Eld Mountain, hiding its bare, terrible peak. Maelga welcomed them, laughing and crying over them, and twisting her curls into wild tufts on her head, and they stayed late with her until the dusk drifted like smoke between the trees and the moon moved through the stars above Eldwold like a silver ship without a mast.

Tam went home finally with his weary guards, and Sybel sat quietly at Maelga's hearth, a cup of hot wine in her hand, her eyes still, looking inward. Maelga rocked in her chair, the rings on her hands catching light from seven candles as they moved back and forth on the arms of the chair. She said finally,

"Such a still land it is without its warlords . . . so confused and childlike. And the Sirle ladies sleep alone tonight, and the children sleep fatherless. Will they come back?"

"I do not know," Sybel murmured. "I do not know anymore the minds of those great beasts. I cannot care. It seems I have heard a dream, except that—no dream could hurt so deeply or be so endless. Maelga, I am like weary earth after the killing, hardening winter . . . I do not know if anything green and living will grow from me again . . ."

"Be gentle with yourself, my white one. Come with me tomorrow through the forest; we will gather black mushrooms and herbs that, crushed against the fingers, give a magic smell. You will feel the sun on your hair and the rich earth beneath your feet, and the fresh winds scented with the spice of snow from the hidden places on Eld Mountain. Be patient, as you must always be patient with new pale seeds buried in the dark ground. When you are stronger, you can begin to think again. But now is the time to feel."

Day and night slid together in a timeless quiet she did not measure until one day she woke to the motionless splash of light on her floor, the voiceless stones rising about her, and a little seed of restlessness woke with her. She wandered through the still house, the empty gardens, stopping at the edge of the swan lake to watch the wild birds feed in it. She circled the lake and went to Gyld's cave where in her mind's eye she saw him lying curled once more in the darkness, his mind-voice whispering into hers. The wet stones surrounded an emptiness that had no voice; she turned away from the silence, went back into the vagrant autumn winds that made their own bright paths across the mountain, leaving her behind.

She went back to the house, sat in the domed room. She began to search again, calling through Eldwold and beyond Eldwold for the Liralen. The hours passed; night winked above her dome, and she sat lost in her calling, feeling the power stir and strengthen in her mind. Near dawn, when the moon had set and the stars had begun to fray in the sky, she woke out of her calling, rose stiffly. She opened the door, stood at the threshold smelling the wet earth and the quiet trees scented and damp in the early morning. Then she saw beyond her open gates Coren dismount, lead his horse into her yard.

She straightened, her throat suddenly dry. He stopped when he saw her, his eyes still, waiting. She drew a breath and found her voice.

"Coren. I was calling the Liralen."

"You called me." He paused, still waiting, and she said,

"Please—come in."

He put his horse in the side room, and came to join her beside her cold hearth. She lit candles in the dimness; the light between them traced the bones and hollows of his face. Memories began to stir in her; she looked away from him quickly.

"Are you hungry? You must have been riding all night. Or did you stay last night at Mondor?"

"No. I left Sirle yesterday afternoon." His gaze, insistent on her face, forced her eyes upward finally, to meet his. His voice lost a little of its aloofness. "You are so thin. What have you been doing?"

"I do not know. Little things, I think—sewing, gardening, looking for herbs with Maelga . . . Then, yesterday, for the first time I began to hear how silent my house is, how empty. And so I began to call again. I did—I did not mean to disturb you."

"I did not mean to be disturbed. When I woke that morning and found you gone, I did not think I would ever hear your voice tugging at me again. My brothers were angry with me for quarreling with you; they said that was why you left: because I was being unreasonable."

"That was not why I ran."

"I know."

Her hands closed on the arms of her chair. She whispered, her eyes wide on his face, "What do you know?"

He looked away from her then, to the empty hearth. "I guessed," he said wearily. "Not that morning, but later, in the slow, quiet days while I waited for my brothers to return. I heard reports of Drede's strange, sudden death, of the warlords of Eldwold vanishing on their way to war. The land was buzzing of impossible things: of bright animals, ancient names, half-forgotten tales. The war had been taken away from us as easily as you take a game from a child. I remembered then the riddle Cyrin gave you the day he came to Sirle. It was the same riddle he gave to me before I saw Rommalb. I should have warned you, but I did not think then that there was any need for you to be afraid. And, remembering that, I knew what must have happened to you. You would not have given up that war for me, or for Tamlorn, or for anyone you loved. You would have had what you wanted, except you made one mistake: holding Rommalb, you neglected to give it what it required of you."

She was silent a long moment. Then she whispered, her face lowered, half-hidden from him, "You are wise, Coren. I gave up everything in return for my life, and then I ran. I ran in my mind past the borders of it, because I had nowhere else to go. Tam came to find me. He woke me. If he had not come—I do not know what would have happened to me." She lifted her head, looked at him as he stared, his face closed from her, into the hearth. She said wistfully, "If you are still angry with me, why did you come? You did not have to answer my lonely voice. I did not expect to see you again."

He stirred. "I did not expect to come. But how could I know you were here in this empty house without Tam, or your animals, or even me, and not come? You did not need me before, and I do not know if you want me now, but I heard you and I had to come."

Her brows drew together. She said softly, a little puzzledly, "If you heard the voice in me that calls you without my knowing, then you must know I need you."

"You have told me you needed me before; it is easy to say. But that night, when Rommalb came to you in the darkness—you did not even need me then to hold you, as you held me once on this hearth, before you even loved me."

She gazed at him, her lips parted. She smiled suddenly, and realized then how long it had been since she had laughed. She hid the smile like a precious secret, her head bent, and said gravely, "I wanted to wake you, but you seemed so far from me—"

"That is easy to say, too. You did not need me when Mithran called you, or when you plotted your revenge with Rok, or even when Rommalb threatened your life. You go your own way always, and I never know what you are thinking, what you are going to do. And now you are laughing at me. I did not come all this way from Sirle to have you laugh at me."

She shook her hair back, the blood bright in her face. She slipped her hand over his and felt his fingers turn to close automatically around it. "I am sorry. But Coren, that is what I need you for now. I have fought for myself—and fought myself. But there is no joy in that. It is only when I am with you that I know, deep in me, how to laugh, and there is no one, no one who can teach me that but you."

He gazed at her, his mouth crooked in the beginnings of a reluctant smile. "Is that all you need me for?"

She shook her head, the laughter fading. "No," she whispered. "I need you to forgive me. And then perhaps I can begin to forgive myself. There is no one but you who can do that either."

She heard the draw of his breath. "Sybel, I almost could not do that. I carried anger and pain like a stone in me: anger with you and Rok and even Drede, even after he died, because you had thought more about him those days than me. Then one night I saw my face in a dream: a dark, sour face with no love, no laughter in it, and I woke in the dark with my heart pounding against my ribs, because it was not my face but Drede's."

"No—you will never look like Drede."

"Drede was young once, and he loved a woman. She hurt him and he never forgave her, so he died frightened and alone. It frightened me that I could so easily make that same mistake with you. Sybel, will you forgive me?"

She smiled, his face blurred under her eyes. "For what? There is nothing."

"For being afraid to tell you that I love you. For being afraid to ask you to come back to Sirle with me."

Her head bowed, her fingers so tight in his hand that she felt the lock of their bones. "I am afraid, too, of myself. But Coren, I do not want to stay here and watch you go away from me. I need you. I need to love you. Please ask me to come with you. Please."

"Will you come?"

"Oh, yes. Yes. Thank you."

He reached out with his free hand, turned her face upward. "Sybel, do not cry. Please."

"I cannot help it."

"You are making me cry."

"I cannot help that either. Coren, I have not laughed or cried for so long, and today, before the sun has even risen, with you I have done both."

He pulled her toward him. They slid to the floor, and the candle, knocked over, extinguished itself against the stone in the first ray of sunlight. She hid her face against him, feeling, as she wept, his hands smoothing her hair, cupping her face as he whispered broken, soothing words. Then for a long time they were wordless, until the light, tracing a fine web through Coren's hair, fell on Sybel's eyes and she opened them, blinking. She stirred, stiff, and Coren loosed her reluctantly. She smiled, looking into his tired, bloodless face, her own eyes lined with weariness.

"Are you hungry?"

He nodded, smiling. "I will cook something for us. Sybel, it is so strange to come here and not see Cyrin looking at me out of his red eyes, or Gules Lyon melting around a corner."

"Tam said he heard a song about you and Cyrin, and your brothers."

He laughed, a touch of color in his face. "I heard it, too. Oh, Sybel, think of six grown men, twice as many seasoned warlords and an odd number of messengers and armor-bearers gathered in the dawn to overthrow a King and suddenly, without a second thought, riding after a great Boar with marble tusks gleaming like quarter-moons, and bristles like silver sparks, who beckoned with his eyes full of some secret knowledge so that we followed like a group of beardless boys following the beckoning of a street-woman's eyes. Harpists will sing of us for centuries, and we will lie burning in our graves. I woke to myself in Mirkon Forest and saw a chain of riders disappearing into the trees after a moon-colored Boar, and I realized suddenly who that Boar was. So I went home and five women met me at the door weeping, and not one of them for me. They said the Sirle army was bewildered, leaderless, and messengers had been pounding at their doors all morning, demanding to know what to do. Then we began to hear tales of Cat and Swan and Dragon from all over Eldwold. My brothers began to straggle home after seven days and for once in his life Eorth had no words in him. And Rok—the Lion of Sirle aged ten years on that ride. He still has not been able to speak of it. It was like a dream; the endless ride, the great, elusive Boar always just ahead, just ahead. . . . Sybel, I woke to myself and I was bone-hungry and whipped by branches and so weary I wanted to cry, and my horse had not even raised a sweat. . . ." He shook his head. "You can weave your life so long—only so long, and then a thing in the world out of your control will tug at one vital thread and leave you patternless and subdued."

"I know. When I let those great animals go I did not dream they would do that one last thing for me. I miss them."

"Perhaps they will return to you someday, missing the sound of your voice speaking their names. By then we will have a houseful of wizardlings to care for them like Tam did." He got up stiffly from the cold stones, helped her rise. She stood close to him, looking around at her empty house.

"Yes. I need a child now that Tam is no longer a child. Coren . . ."

"What?"

"Please—I do not want to spend another night in

this house. I know you are tired, and so is your horse, but—will you take me home now?"

His arms circled her. "My White Lady," he whispered. "I have waited so long for you to want to come to me, White one, my Liralen . . ."

"Am I that to you?" she said wonderingly. "I have given you as much trouble as that white bird is giving me. I have been so close to you and yet so far . . ." Her voice drifted away; she was silent, listening to the pattern of her words. Coren looked down at her.

"What are you thinking?"

She murmured vaguely. Old memories blossomed, faded in her mind, of her first callings of the Liralen, of Mithran's words, of the last dream of it, where it lay broken in the depths of her mind. She drew a sharp breath, pulling away from Coren.

"Sybel— What?"

"I know—" Her hand closed tightly around his arm; she pulled him to her threshold. He followed, bewildered, looked over her head into the empty yard. Then she said, her voice taut, unfamiliar, "Blammor," and his face jerked back to her.

"What are you doing?" he breathed. The Blammor came to them, the mist of a shadow between the great pines, its moon-colored, sightless eyes white as the snow-buried peak of Eld. Sybel looked into its eyes, gathering her thoughts, but before she could speak to it, the dark lines of it grew mist-colored, molding a form. The fluid crystal of its eyes melted downward, curving into white, clean lines: a long, flute-slender neck, a white curve of breast like a snow-touched hill, a broad sweep of snowy back, and long, trailing, pennant-shaped wings that brushed the soft ground like trains of finest wool. A sound broke sharply from Coren. The great bird looked down at them, taller than either of them, gentle and beautiful, and its eyes, the Blammor's, were moon-clear. Sybel touched her eyes, feeling the fire burning dry at the back of them. She opened her mind to the bird, and tales murmured beneath its thoughts, ancient and precious as the thin tapestries on the walls of a king's house.

Give me your name.

You have it.

"Liralen," Coren whispered. "The Liralen. Sybel, how did you know? How did you know?"

She reached out to touch it, the feathers strong yet sleek beneath her hand. Tears ran down her face; she brushed them absently. "You gave me a key, when you called me that. I knew then it must be something close to me, yet far . . . and then I remembered that when I called the Liralen so long ago, the Blammor came and told me itself it was not uncalled. And the night it came to me and I nearly died of terror like Drede, I saw deep in me the Liralen dead, and I did not want it dead—that saved my life, because in my sorrow for it I forgot to be afraid. And somehow, the Blammor—the Liralen—knew even better than I how much it meant to me. That is why Mithran could never take it: he knew that he would have to take the Blammor, and that he could never do."

The Liralen's voice drifted into her mind. *You are growing wise, Sybel. I came long ago, but you could not see me. I was always here.*

I know.

How may I serve you?

She looked deep into its eyes. Her hand at rest in Coren's gentle hold, she said softly,

"Please take us home."